All best

The Adventure of the Creeping Man

By Sir Arthur Conan Doyle

*Facsimile edition, with an introduction and
annotated transcription by Neil McCaw*

Supported by

Arthur Conan Doyle

Published by Winchester University Press 2017
Original material copyright © Winchester University Press
Manuscript reprinted with kind permission of The Arthur Conan
Doyle Collection, Lancelyn Green Bequest.

The Conan Doyle Estate Ltd.®

First Published in Great Britain in 2017 by
Winchester University Press
Winchester SO22 4NR

British Library Cataloguing-in-Publication Data
A CIP catalogue record for this book is available
from the British Library.

ISBN: 978-1-906113-24-7

Designed and Typeset by All Caps
Manuscript Photographed by Emily Whiting
Printed and Bound in Great Britain

'Read at once if convenient - if inconvenient read all the same'

Contents

Introduction

Part 1
A Critical History

*T*he *Case-Book of Sherlock Holmes* (1927), Sir Arthur Conan Doyle's final journey into the world of Sherlock Holmes, is also the least critically well-regarded of all the Holmes short story collections. The tales within it, including 'The Adventure of the Creeping Man', have been dissected and critiqued with a degree of negativity absent in critical discussions of *The Adventures, The Memoirs, and The Return*[1]. Take, for instance, Colin Dexter's introduction to the facsimile edition of 'The Adventure of the Lion's Mane'; now, perhaps the editors of the volume assumed that crime-writer Dexter would feel obliged to offer sympathetic comment on the story, perhaps they were thinking that the prestige of his contribution would outweigh all other considerations, but nevertheless, it must have stung more than a little to receive such a damning indictment of the story – 'a strong contender for being adjudged the worst in the whole of the Sherlock Holmes corpus'.[2]

Most negative assessments of 'The Adventure of the Creeping Man' itself are rooted in one or more of the following contentions:

(1) That the quality of the writing is not up to Conan Doyle's usual standard.
(2) That (an extreme version of critique (1)) Conan Doyle did not in fact write the story and it was instead the product of an unknown 'hack' writer.
(3) That the story is indicative of a writer who is no longer interested in their subject matter.
(4) That there is in the story (as with *The Case-Book* more widely) an unnecessarily graphic cruelty and pessimistic view of human nature that is far from the charm of the earlier, Victorian, Holmes stories.
(5) That the story is more science fiction than detective fiction.

And in this introduction, it is the intention to explore the nature and validity of each of these criticisms, in order to assess the extent to which the current critical reputation of 'The Creeping Man' is truly justified.

That the quality of the writing is not up to Conan Doyle's usual standard

Conan Doyle has rarely been considered a 'literary' writer. Indeed, even during his lifetime, when he was desperate to be best known for his sprawling, multi-volume, painstakingly-researched historical fictions, the overwhelming proportion of critics and readers saw him primarily as a purveyor of popular fiction. And this reputation for popular rather than high-cultural writings has stayed with him, demonstrated as recently as the first decade of the twenty-first century, when the British government refused to place a protection order on one of Doyle's previous homes, Undershaw, with an implied whiff of literary snobbery in its suggestion that the writer did not 'occupy a significant enough position in the nation's consciousness'.[3]

The difference between such wider cultural elitism and the specific criticism of *The Case-Book,* however, is that the attack on the quality of the final Holmes stories is a relative one – it suggests that Conan Doyle's writing was *worse* in this collection than it had been in previous incarnations of the Great Detective; which is obviously a difficult critique to rebuff without getting caught up in an interminably subjective game of one-story-versus-another. Readers might, for instance, in countering such a suggestion, point to the writerly high points of 'The Creeping Man', such as Watson's wonderfully comic diagnosis of Professor Presbury's extraordinary behavior ('Lumbago, possibly'[4]), or the fact that the story features some of the detective's most memorable pithiness – 'Come at once if convenient – if inconvenient come all the same'.[5] But beyond such quantitative/qualitative to-ing and fro-ing between earlier and later Holmes stories, the whole question as to which material is more accomplished lacks any sustainable interest – especially as the idea that Conan Doyle's writing was no longer quite as sharp as it once had been when he was in his 30s and striving to carve out an identity and a voice as a writer, now that he was a very rich and very comfortable man approaching his 70s, is hardly contentious.

That Conan Doyle did not in fact write the story and it was instead the product of an unknown 'hack' writer

For some critics the supposed weaknesses of the stories in *The Case-Book* is only explained by the notion that Conan Doyle did not in fact write them; this is a suggestion on the lines of other literary conspiracy theories that doubt the official story of authorship, most famously in the case of Shakespeare, whose plays are variously attributed to the 17th Earl of Oxford, Christopher Marlowe, Francis Bacon, or the 6th Earl of Derby. And, just as is the case with Shakespeare, there is no credible evidence that Conan Doyle did not write any of his most well-known works either. Instead, there are a hotchpotch of dubious critical assumptions that imply a belief that there is a characteristic essence to every Sherlock Holmes story, and thus any that appears to lack this essence could only have been written by someone else.

Versions of this position have been articulated by D. Martin Dakin, who in his *A Sherlock Holmes Commentary* alludes to 'the problem of *The Case-Book*'[6] and notes his 'doubts about some of these cases',[7] and also by W.W. Robson, who claims the stories were originally sent to Doyle so he could 'have adapted them'.[8] This, we are told, is the only feasible explanation of the fact that 'it is hard to believe that any careful reader...would be prepared to testify that they all came from the pen of Conan Doyle'.[9] Robson's judgement is rooted in a conviction that the prose in tales such as 'The Creeping Man' is unusually vulgar, featuring slang and supposedly 'non-literary' writing. And the accusation that somehow the later stories don't measure up to the rest has gained a lot of traction – even being regurgitated in Nicholas Meyer's pastiche *The Seven-Per-Cent Solution* (1976), in which Meyer's 'Watson' talks of 'two of the cases I penned concerning Holmes [which] were total fabrications',[10] and then alludes to Holmesian 'forgeries by other hands than mine, which include such drivel as "The Lion's Mane", "The Mazarin Stone", "The Creeping Man", and "The Three Gables".'[11] However, the fact that this 'conspiracy' of authorship ended up being spoofed within a Holmesian pastiche is hardly encouraging to any conviction as to its validity.

That the story is indicative of a writer who is no longer interested in their subject matter
Another accusation levelled at the stories in *The Case-Book* is that they illustrate how, by the 1920s, Arthur Conan Doyle had lost his enthusiasm for his Great Detective. David Stuart Davies, for one, notes how 'by this late stage in his career, Doyle had little interest in his greatest creation',[12] noting how 'his heart was not in it'.[13] Davies goes on to cite the critic John Gore's view that *The Case-Book* as a whole was 'a waste-paper recycling job, an exhausted performance'.[14] A similar point-of-view is also evident in Michael Hardwick's *The Complete Guide to Sherlock Holmes* (1986), in which, whilst acknowledging that the last collection showed 'some gleams of the old brilliance', Hardwick concludes that it was so far 'below the old standard that the provenance of some of them has been called into question'.[15] He doesn't quite relegate 'The Creeping Man' into the very lowest division of stories (that is reserved for 'The Adventure of the Blanched Soldier', 'The Adventure of the Three Gables', and 'The Adventure of the Lion's Mane', which he labels 'sub-standard works...displaying many Americanisms of language and style'[16]), but his overall view is that it is still 'another out of the tin box, but one which, unfortunately, might as well have been left there'.[17]

It is unarguable that Doyle's attitude towards Sherlock Holmes in later life was indifferent. This is born out in many of his letters, as well as his autobiography. However, the question here is not so much whether he was indifferent, but whether and how this attitude *particularly* influenced the later Holmes stories. Because if we are to agree that this was an issue specific to this final collection, then we also must be convinced that Doyle's earlier Holmes stories were all the product of passion, enthusiasm and dedication to the Holmesian cause; as such we can then judge the final collection to be a notable dropping off in standards. And the problem with such an interpretation of Conan Doyle's career is that anyone who knows anything about his testy and complex relationship with his most famous fictional creation knows only too well that relatively early in his writing career he had already started to lose interest in, and passion for, writing about Holmes: 'After I had done two series...I saw that I was in danger of having my hand forced, and of being entirely identified with what I regarded as a lower stratum of literary achievement.'[18] This growing alienation from his most famous creation then became so pronounced, as all Sherlockians know, that he ended up catapulting Holmes off the Reichenbach Falls, locked in a deadly embrace with his arch-enemy Professor Moriarty. This, he saw at the time, as bringing to an end what he (even at that relatively early stage) had come to see as his incarceration within the role of the author of Sherlock Holmes.

What this illustrates is that Conan Doyle's relationship with Holmes was problematic pretty much from the outset. Most of his enthusiasm for the character burnt out after the first two novellas and the initial collection of short stories. As such, it is simply not convincing to argue that somehow *The Case-Book* betrays a unique dip in writerly interest and conviction. As Doyle himself acknowledged, he had started to see his Sherlock Holmes stories solely in terms of their financial rewards long before that: 'I buried my banking account along with him.'[19] It is feasible to argue that by the end of his writing career Conan Doyle saw Holmes almost *entirely* within the context of monetary remuneration, a way of facilitating his Spiritualist campaigning, or his house renovations, or his purchase of the latest gadget or technological advance. But the very most anyone can seriously claim is that this sense of pragmatism reached its apotheosis with *The Case-Book* – the general attitude of indifference had been there pretty much all along.

That there is in the story (as with *The Case-Book* more widely) an unnecessarily graphic cruelty and pessimistic view of human nature that is far from the charm of the earlier, Victorian, Holmes stories

Some of the negative criticism of the stories within *The Case-Book* also mentions the supposedly uncharacteristic, bleak tone and vision of the stories. They depict twentieth-century humanity, it is claimed, with a harshness absent from the earlier material, and focus almost relentlessly on human mean-spiritedness, lack of charity, and brutality. The stories are, we are told, 'disappointing in construction and surprising in their unpleasantness', and this grows out of 'the dark and cruel nature of their content'.[20]

But Holmes readers know that this quality is not unique to this final collection. There are moments in earlier Sherlock Holmes stories that are at least as bleak as those within *The Case-Book* – 'The Adventure of the Cardboard Box', for instance, a story written more than three decades earlier, features a jealous husband who removes the ears of his wife and her lover after he has murdered them, and then posts them to his sister-in-law, who he believes culpable for the affair that ruined his marriage. And it would be difficult to imagine a more existentially pessimistic statement as that which features at the conclusion of that story: 'What is the meaning of it, Watson...? What object is served by this circle of misery and violence and fear? It must tend to some end, or else our universe is ruled by chance, which is unthinkable. But what end? There is the great standing perennial problem to which human reason is as far from an answer as ever.'[21]

Having said that, it is certainly the case that a number of the tales within the final Holmes collection are themselves heavy with pessimism. Yet, surely, it would be remarkable if they were not. For *The Case-Book of Sherlock Holmes* is separated from all of the other Holmes short-story collections not just by the passing of time, but rather the passing of a very specific period of time – the tumultuous and traumatic years of World War I, which concluded less than a decade before its publication. It was, as such, shaped by the aftermath of this conflict. What critics have called the 'emotional misery and physical pain' of the stories is the boot-print of 'the horrors of the war',[22] the spectre of more than 700,000 British lives lost during the fighting or afterwards, including Conan Doyle's own brother and son. Within this context the 'ruthless realism' and 'gallery of monstrosity and cruelty'[23] of stories such as 'The Adventure of the Creeping Man,' should be seen as consequences of war. Readers readily accept the fact that other literature of this period, such as D. H. Lawrence's *Women in Love* (1920) and Virginia Woolf's *Mrs Dalloway* (1925), should be interpreted in terms of the legacy of conflict, but seem somehow to be less open to affording Conan Doyle that same courtesy, and viewing the later Holmes stories in terms of this wider cultural-historical frame. What Robson categorises as Conan Doyle's tendency towards 'the gruesomeness of Edgar Allan Poe'[24] in these stories is not simply an echo of a past literary genre; rather it is a manifestation of profound cultural and psychological trauma. Through his fiction Doyle was trying to come to terms with the increasingly 'cruel, disenchanted post-war world'.[25]

The problem, for some Holmesian readers, seems to be that such a sensibility does not sit well with their expectations of the Great Detective; it jars with the familiar cosiness of

Baker Street and the Victorian charm of the world in which Holmes and Watson had previously plied their trade. And indeed, it is fair to say that often *The Case-Book* does lack some of the cultural nostalgia of the earlier, pre-World War I material, especially those stories that had fixed Sherlock Holmes in a Victorian world of shadowed gaslit streets, etiquette and moral reserve – a world warmly encapsulated in Vincent Starrett's '221b' poem, where 'it is always eighteen ninety-five'.[26] However, these same readers must also concede that it is entirely out of the question that during the 1920s Conan Doyle could have written as if nothing had happened since those earlier stories. Even if he had consciously striven to pickle Holmes in aspic, tell-tale signs of the temper of these new times and the aftermath of the brutality of international conflict were sure to have punctured some of the comfortable complacency of the idealised Holmesian world.

That the story is more science fiction than detective fiction[27]

For some readers, the main problem with 'The Adventure of the Creeping-Man' is that, in the words of Leslie Klinger, the story is 'more of a science-fiction story than a mystery'.[28] Others, including Stuart Davies, take this further, accusing Conan Doyle not just of writing science fiction, but rather of writing it *badly*, attacking the way the story 'veers towards risible science fiction'.[29] In so doing these critics do two things; first, they imply that there is an inherent incompatibility between Holmesian detective stories and the science-fiction genre, as if somehow a Holmesian *essence* risks being diluted. Second, and this is particularly the case with Davies, they cast doubt on the accuracy and effectiveness of Conan Doyle's writing, and especially his depiction of youth-regenerative science.

And if we are being fair, it is certainly true that there is much in 'The Creeping Man' that feels to a modern reader like an extraordinary leap of the imagination. Conan Doyle's portrayal of the hormone-addled Professor Presbury, leaping 'from branch to branch...sure of foot and firm of grasp, climbing apparently in mere joy at his own powers',[30] stretches the boundaries of what is credible. However, this same modern reader needs to be very careful to avoid *presentism*,[31] the anachronistic judgement of the supposed eccentricities of the past. For in reality, there is nothing in 'The Creeping Man' that is notably out-of-keeping with the way later-nineteenth- and earlier-twentieth-century science fiction explored, often in a bizarre fashion, scientific experimentation. Take, for instance, the way that H.G. Wells depicts vivisection in *The Island of Dr Moreau* (1896); this is a novel in which unusual science leads to the creation, through a perverse grafting of animal parts onto alternative host bodies, of a leopard-man, hyena-swine, dog-man, satyr-man, fox-bear witch, half-finished puma woman, and a range of other 'Beast Folk':

> The population of the island, Montgomery informed me, now numbered rather more than sixty of these strange creations of Moreau's art, not counting the smaller monstrosities which lived in the undergrowth and were without human form. Altogether he had made nearly a hundred and twenty; but many had died, and others—like the writhing Footless Thing of which he had told me—had come by violent ends.[32]

These elements of Wells's novel also stretch the boundaries of the credible, especially when viewed through a twenty-first-century lens, and to represent science in a way that feels simplistic, even crass at times. But this has to be seen in context; since the later nineteenth century scientific exploration has developed at an extraordinary pace. Readers now routinely understand aspects of scientific knowledge to an extent that would have been inconceivable back then. Thus, what should matter to a modern reader is not whether the science of a story from the past feels right to them based on what they know *now*, but rather whether the accuracy of the scientific speculations described had a broad basis in truth during the *writer's own* times. In that light, *The Island of Dr Moreau* is a graphic refraction of later Victorian attitudes towards science and evolution at a time when people were starting to become ever more concerned with animal welfare, illustrated by the passing of legislation attempting to limit cruelty to animals through experimentation in 1876. The scientific credibility of the novel thus in part comes through its engagement with these concerns regarding vivisection, and the wider social and political process through which (for just one example) the British Union for the Abolition of Vivisection was created in 1898.

In a comparable way, Conan Doyle's 'The Creeping Man' was also informed by its ethical-scientific context. It is, after all, a twentieth-century version of the familiar myth of the Fountain of Youth, a myth that can be traced back to the fifth century BC writings of Herodotus at least. Indeed, the 'water/elixir of life' or 'eternal life' oral tale is a stock element of many cultures, such as the story of the 'Philosopher's stone'. The human quest to fight the process of ageing has a very long cultural history. But beyond the broader symbolic dimensions of the story, 'The Creeping Man' has a far more direct, explicit connection to actual developments in rejuvenative science during the earlier twentieth century. For these are the backdrop of the depiction of the travails of the central character, Professor Presbury. Presbury is the means through which Conan Doyle confronts the central scientific question at the heart of the story – whether it is feasible, or desirable, to rejuvenate the human body through the transplantation of body materials from other species. And through the narrative of Presbury's dalliance with alternative science Doyle makes his own contribution to the debate about the role man might play within the process of evolution, and in particular in relation to what Darwin called the 'means of modification and coadaptation'.[33]

A significant reason why this debate had become so topical was that ever since the last decades of the nineteenth century, people had begun to ask questions as to the nature, and direction, of the evolutionary process. The key principles of Charles Darwin's *On the Origin of Species,* first published in 1859, had become ever more influential. And in the minds of many, the principles of evolutionary thinking fed inevitably into an assumption that over time the human species would naturally progress. And yet, the realities of British experience from the later Victorian period onwards jarred with such an assumption, with foreign policy bloody noses in the Sudan and South Africa, a growing panic about a perceived outbreak of criminality and the supposed discovery of criminal genetics (first defined in the work of Lombroso), and social changes that for some threatened the long-held values and assumptions on which Victorian society had been built, including the emergence of the 'New Woman'. And the result of all this was that the self-aggrandising and national posturing of the 1851 Great Exhibition of the Work of All Nations and its aftermath seemed less appropriate, and this eventually gave way to doubts about the nature of the future, captured in Max Nordau's *Degeneration* (1892): 'The disposition of the times is curiously confused, a compound of feverish restlessness and blunted discouragement, of fearful presage and hang-dog renunciation.'[34]

The emerging contradiction between an evolutionary assumption of progress and the lived experience of the later nineteenth and earlier twentieth centuries resulted in a growing interest in theories such as eugenics, which was favoured by thinkers such as Francis Galton, writers such as Wells and George Bernard Shaw, and political leaders such as Arthur Balfour. They argued that if national disaster was to be avoided, human beings had to take a more active, interventionist role in the evolutionary process, and (they believed as a consequence) participation in human reproduction should be limited to those with the greatest abilities. This explains why the theme of human proactive involvement in evolutionary development features so often in literature of this period. And why, although on the surface 'The Creeping Man' might appear to be no more than a tale about an ageing man trying to restore his sexual vitality for a younger lover, more fundamentally it is about a human dissatisfaction with the 'normal' evolutionary process, and a desire, as a consequence, to intervene to man's own advantage. It is an implied recognition that old age, in the words of W. H. Curtis in 1906, 'is never physiological, but pathological.'[35]

In terms of the specific science of the story, Conan Doyle was writing at a time when endocrinology was becoming an established branch of knowledge. Owing to the discoveries of men such as Arnold Berthold, who linked hormones and behavioural and sexual characteristics, and Charles Brown-Séquard, developing a so-called 'elixir of life', it was a period of rapid development. Testosterone was eventually isolated in 1935, but prior to that the work of the Austrian scientist Eugen Steinach (1861–1944), who developed an operational procedure whereby the male seminal ducts were vasoligated so as to restore male youth and vitality, and the Russian Serge Voronoff (1866–1951), whose most well-known work was in the field of xenotransplantation, was groundbreaking – if also extremely expensive and only available to a select group of patients. Steinach was reported to have had celebrity clients including Sigmund Freud and W. B. Yeats, and Voronoff achieved notoriety as 'the famous doctor who inserts monkey glands into millionaires'.[36]

The career of Voronoff is particularly relevant to Conan Doyle's story. He supposedly transplanted ape tissue into more than 2,000 male patients with the aim of achieving youthful rejuvenation, and his scientific career was founded in a desire to reverse the assumption that 'among the vertebrate animals...as organic complexity and perfection increase, length of life diminishes'.[37] He was convinced that there was 'some innate peculiarity of the make-up of certain of our organs which have a direct influence on the duration of our life, and which insure our existence for a longer or shorter period'.[38] This was why he developed the techniques honed during an early-career experiment implanting a chimpanzee thyroid gland into a young boy with learning difficulties[39] into a 'rejuvenation' procedure that utilised monkey glands, which was first successfully trialled in 1920.[40] By 1923 the popularity of this procedure was such that a monkey reserve was set up in Africa to ensure that there would always be a ready supply of the animals,[41] and Voronoff became much celebrated in the popular press in articles with titles such as 'Doctor offers cure for age',[42] 'Voronoff performs 1,300 gland grafts',[43] and 'Sex glands for criminals'.[44] By the end of the decade his name had become synonymous in many parts of the world[45] not just with a single scientific procedure, but rather with the whole idea of body rejuvenation, making him a prominent name in the so-called 'life-extensionist' movement.[46]

Consequently, we can see that 'The Adventure of the Creeping Man' is much more than 'risible science fiction'. Certainly, at the very least we must agree with Charles Meyer's assessment that the plot is 'certainly plausible'.[47] For the very particular brand of experimental science that Professor Presbury makes use of was both topical, and indeed feasible at the time the story was written; it also foreshadows subsequent developments in endocrinology. Perhaps unsurprisingly, as a medical man himself, Doyle displays an insightful grasp of the specific science, and also of the wider controversy surrounding its application; almost as if he had knowledge of the fact that many unfavourable media stories were circulating during that period which discussed Voronoff's work in a negative way, often characterising him as a quack or charlatan. And these tended to focus on the more sensational elements of this emerging scientific practice, such as the question as to whether 'people or their children would start devolving into primate behaviour'.[48] The infamy of this science is reflected in Professor Presbury's secretive behaviour, his clandestine attempts to obtain monkey gland extract from outside England, and in the shady character 'Dorak', who deals monkey serum from the shadowy fringes of the continent.

Finally, beyond its informed reflection on the particular cultural and scientific context, and its status as an important landmark in the popular-fictional representation and understanding of xenotransplantation, 'The Creeping Man' also attempts to engage with the ethically and philosophically complex question of whether human beings should intervene in the evolutionary process. This comes, most explicitly, when Sherlock Holmes attempts to offer his own clear and unambiguous moral condemnation of such: 'When one tries to rise above nature one is liable to fall below it. The highest type of man may revert to the animal if he leaves the straight road of destiny'.[49] But the problem with this is that morality is not always compatible with a logical, scientific *modus operandi,* and as a consequence Holmes ends up tying himself in knots. Because whilst it might morally be feasible for him to argue that the experiments of the deviant scientist 'Lowenstein' represent a 'very real danger to humanity,'[50] and that as a consequence any patients who undergo such scientific processes to prolong what he dismissively calls their 'worthless lives' are examples of the 'survival of the least fit,'[51] for Darwin the question of evolutionary survival was not a moral one. Rather, it was dictated by the effectiveness of each species in adaptation. With that in mind, far from being the 'least fit,' any patient who utilised Lowenstein's science to prolong their life could be seen as adapting to their environment successfully; further, if they were then to procreate, furthering their newly-adapted genes into succeeding generations, then they might more accurately be defined as the 'fittest' of the species.

All of which means that in trying to use Holmes to warn against supposedly 'unnatural' scientific practices, Conan Doyle in fact ends up ensnaring him in the ethical complexities of the question as to whether man should have a role in the evolutionary process. And, like many others before him and since, the Great Detective struggles to articulate an unambiguous position on the subject. Which, of all the many things that have been said over the years about 'The Adventure of the Creeping Man,' is for us mere mortals one of the most comforting.

Left, Conan Doyle outside Bush Villas in 1911; Right, the early-career Dr Conan Doyle.
(Published with permission, The Arthur Conan Doyle Collection, Lancelyn Green Bequest)

Part 2
'The Creeping Man' Manuscript

*T*he original manuscript of 'The Adventure of the Creeping Man' sits within a modest, hard-backed, hand-lined exercise book, measuring 16.7cm x 20.4cm. The text is hand-written in Conan Doyle's familiar cursive. Yet, as unostentatious as the manuscript is, reading it still somehow feels different to reading one of the many mass-published versions of the same text. The original handwritten copy has what Walter Benjamin called an 'aura',[52] an indefinable quality that implies a closer, more intimate link between the reader and the writer. One has to be wary, when reading through it, to avoid fetishizing the original as if it were a museum artefact, rather than the potential starting point for a fresh investigation into Conan Doyle's story. Manuscripts might well be historical landmarks, but they are also opportunities to better comprehend the writing/artistic process, to look at different versions of the supposedly *same* text and to gain insight on the nature of that process, with the writing evolving, dynamic and shifting. This is what the textual critic John Bryant calls the 'fluid' text that develops 'In multiple material versions due to revisions (authorial, editorial, cultural).'[53]

So, when we look at an original manuscript we are reminded that we are looking at but one stage in the process(es) of writing, revising, editing, and publishing. There were versions of the text *before* the one we are looking at, even if in some instances these versions only exist in the mind of the writer, and there are versions *after* the one we are looking at. Through reading Conan Doyle's handwritten version of 'The Adventure of the Creeping Man' and the edits and corrections he made, and then placing that alongside the version that ultimately appeared in *The Strand Magazine* – tidied up, smoothed over, and polished – we as readers start to understand the dynamic quality of this short story over time. The gap between the different versions is an implied narrative of the process through which an original idea becomes a best-selling publication. And acknowledging this means pushing past the delimiting idea that texts exist only 'in print and linearly,' and are 'immutable, with one word occupying its given position in a line, and the same word occupying the same space in all copies'.[54] Instead we are forced to concede what Bryant calls the 'fantasy of textual stability.'[55]

Take, for instance, the fact that on the opening page of Conan Doyle's handwritten manuscript of 'The Adventure of the Creeping Man' the narrator tells us that the events commenced 'One Sunday evening early in September of the year 1902'. Whereas, readers of published versions of the story know full well that the line is (and has always been) 'One Sunday evening early in September of the year 1903'. Now, although the poignancy of this change might escape all but the most avid of Sherlockians, the truth is that within the wider world of Sherlockian folklore, and in particular within the context of what enthusiasts call 'the Game' – the ongoing willing suspension of disbelief wherein the characters and events of the stories are treated as if they were real – this difference is of some moment. For, ever since the first Holmesian scholarship, readers and critics have set out to establish an authoritative timeline of the Great Detective's life and adventures. It was a readerly trend initiated by William S. Baring-Gould's *The Chronological Holmes* (1955).[56] Since then, numerous scholars have offered their own Holmesian chronologies, to the extent that questions as to precisely when each Holmes story took place are hotly debated. One of the interesting things about this debate, however, is that there has always been something of a consensus as to the chronological position of 'The Adventures of the Creeping Man' within the Holmesian canon. Baring-Gould placed it as the very last of Holmes's adventures before his retirement to the Sussex coast to keep bees, and so has pretty much everyone else.[57] 'The Creeping Man' is as such seen as a bookend to Holmes's official career as a consulting detective, serving as the fictional gateway not just to the small number of tales that Conan Doyle wrote about Holmes's life post-retirement, but also to that wider world of pastiche fiction and adaptation in which a host of other writers have re-imagined Holmes's later years, most recently in the *Mr Holmes* (2015) film adaptation of Mitch Cullin's novel *A Slight Trick of the Mind* (2005), starring Sir Ian McKellen.

Consequently, the fact that in his handwritten manuscript Conan Doyle sets the narrative in the autumn of 1902 rather than of 1903, is noteworthy. If that date had persisted in all subsequent editions of the story, then the implied narrative of Sherlock Holmes's life and career across the entirety of the stories, would have been different. It would have changed our understanding of 'The Creeping Man,' possibly in a negative way in that the adventure would no longer be seen as a significant moment in his detective career; which would also have had the knock-on effect of enhancing the reputation of one of the other later Holmes stories, as this would then have become 'Holmes's last [official] case.' Which, for stories such as 'Shoscombe Old Place,' 'The Mazarin Stone,' and 'The Three Gables' (the most likely candidates for such a 'promotion') would have meant a significant boost in reputation, after years of often negative critical comment.

Of the other most notable differences between Conan Doyle's manuscript and later published versions of 'The Creeping Man,' many of these are revealing of the writer's particular writing process, and how he worked to create dramatic effect for his readers. Thus, on page four of the manuscript we notice him developing the characteristics of the dog that is to be at the heart of the story, striking out the original version of 'Roy' the playful little spaniel, and then rewriting him as a giant wolf-hound. Which at first seems perfectly understandable, bearing in mind we know that at the end of the narrative this hound will attack and almost kill Professor Presbury, and it is thus hard to believe that utilising a relatively modest spaniel for the purpose would have worked successfully. However, the logic of this change only seems unarguable because we come to the manuscript already familiar (probably) with the ending of the story. If for a second we put this knowledge aside, then the fact that Conan Doyle had ever thought that a small spaniel would be dramatically appropriate in this role seems extremely odd. Which then legitimately makes us suspect that perhaps the precise details of the narrative conclusion had not been worked out before Conan Doyle began writing the story; as such, it was fine for 'Roy' to be a loyal spaniel at that point because all he was being asked to do was show hostility towards his owner. But as soon as Doyle decided that the dog was going to mount an almost fatal attack on the Professor, a greater physical presence and ferocity was required for this to be believable, and so the breed and nature of the dog had to be changed. So Doyle decided to add in a version of the dog much more in keeping with the Gothic beasts of other Holmes stories, such as *The Hound of the Baskervilles* and the mastiff 'Carlo' that attacks Jephro Rucastle at the conclusion of 'The Copper Beeches'.

But this is not the only instance where having access to Conan Doyle's original manuscript enables the reader to have a better understanding of the development of the Gothic drama of the text. This is also apparent in the way the author changed some of the plot details, such as amending the source of the implanted monkey gland serum from Paris to Prague. This might at first appear inconsequential, but this did not happen for no reason. Perhaps, on reflection, Doyle deemed 'Paris' too cultured, or too much an accessible part of the modern world, to be seen as the home of such deviant, outlandish scientific practices. So, he relocated this science to Bohemia, and was thus able to draw on the very different image of 'Prague' in the minds of his 1920s readers. Prague offers something much darker, something certainly more geographically remote, and these characteristics, alongside its Gothic heritage, might have seemed more in tune with the implied world of dubious medical experimentation.

Perhaps the largest number of amendments to the handwritten manuscript are those wherein Conan Doyle revises his story so as to sharpen the way the narrative builds and better sustains the tension and drama. Early on, for instance, he softens his description of Professor Presbury, removing mention of his 'haggard' features so as not to draw quite so much attention to him, which then allows for a more incremental build-up towards the eventual realisation of what has taken place. It is also likely that this was the reason for the deletion of all specific mentions of Presbury's ape-like hands and knuckles in the early part of the story, only for them to be added in later on when the drama was reaching its high point.

In examining the manuscript in this way it is almost as if it comes alive, and we start to understand the various dimensions of Doyle's writerly process. The versions of 'The Adventure of Creeping Man' in this volume should thus be seen as distinct yet interwoven stages in the evolution of 'the text'; and key to grasping this is an awareness that 'the text' is no definitive or fixed entity, but rather it is *all* its parts - 'original manuscripts, proofs, and editions'.[58] Reading an original handwritten edition should not be like gazing in awe at 'the knucklebones of the saints',[59] but rather the means through which we more fully comprehend the entire 'story of revision'[60] within which each text plays a leading, as well as shifting, role.

Part 3

Conan Doyle, Sherlock Holmes and Portsmouth

*T*he manuscript of 'The Adventure of the Creeping Man' is one item out of more than 60,000 that make up 'The Arthur Conan Doyle Collection, Lancelyn Green Bequest'. This Collection is under the custodianship of the city of Portsmouth. It was bequeathed to the city by Richard Lancelyn Green, who was one of the foremost global Sherlockian collectors and experts at the time of his premature death in 2004. He made this decision after having a positive experience at Portsmouth Central Library, where he was researching into Arthur Conan Doyle's years spent in Southsea, a residential area of the city.

Much could be said about Richard himself;[61] there is a wealth of evidence of his fascination with, and dedication to, the global phenomenon of Sherlock Holmes. But the vast breadth and range of the Collection he left behind speaks louder than words. There are many thousands of books, including a mint-condition first edition of the *Beeton's Christmas Annual* that first introduced the Great Detective to the world, as well as hundreds of objects and ephemera related to the original stories, Conan Doyle's life, and the array of adaptations and reworkings of his writings, and many tens of thousands of pieces of archival material to do with the Conan Doyle family and the global culture of Sherlock Holmes – in a multiplicity of languages.

As well as the positive experience Lancelyn Green had whilst in Portsmouth, leaving him well disposed towards the city, there was another underlying motivation for this bequest – the reason he had visited the city in the first place. For Southsea is where Conan Doyle was living when he created Sherlock Holmes, making it the metaphorical birthplace of the world's greatest fictional detective. Doyle arrived in the June of 1882, setting up home at No. 1 Bush Villas, Elm Grove: 'Wedged in between a church and a hotel, so I act as a sort of a buffer.'[62] He arrived, a man in his early 20s, imagined by Dickson Carr as 'a frock-coated figure six feet two inches in height, seeming even taller by reason of its vast breadth, in weight fifteen stone when in training without an ounce of fat'.[63] At the time Southsea, was 'growing, partly as a residential suburb outside the bounds of the old naval fortress (the part of the city still known as Old Portsmouth), and also as a rather genteel watering-place for summer visitors of the middle and upper classes'.[64]

Bush Villa - Southsea

Left, Conan Doyle outside Bush Villas; Right top & bottom, Dr Conan Doyle
during his early career (All published with permission, The Arthur Conan
Doyle Collection, Lancelyn Green Bequest)

The week following his arrival he placed an announcement in the *Portsmouth Evening News*
stating that 'Dr Doyle begs to notify that he has removed to 1, Bush Villas, Elm Grove, next to
the Bush Hotel'.[65] It was a key moment in his life: 'A wonderful thing to have a house of your
own for the first time, however humble it may be.'[66] However, although on arrival he might have
been greeted by a picturesque scene, wherein 'women in large floral hats and flowing crinoline
dresses clutched parasols as they strolled along the pathways of Southsea Common, attended
by gentlemen in boaters',[67] his situation soon became difficult, with the task of establishing a
new medical practice with no prior connections to the area, financially challenging: 'I shall
struggle along somehow. The great thing is to scrape the rent together. I have £5 laid by towards
it. I really hardly know myself how I have managed it.'[68]

Some of our understanding of these early years in Southsea comes to us vicariously, through Doyle's autobiographical novel, *The Stark Munro Letters* (1895), a barely-disguised account of his own early-career experiences. In this we learn that the choice of Portsmouth as a home was largely a pragmatic one: 'It should be some place large enough to give...plenty of room for expansion...not too near London...a place where I know nobody.' The partial anonymity the area afforded him was important, he felt, because although he could 'rough it by myself' he didn't feel able to 'keep up appearances before visitors'.[69] In his later autobiography, Doyle shows himself to have been even more circumspect: 'I finally decided that Portsmouth would be a good place, the only reason being that I knew the conditions at Plymouth, and Portsmouth seemed analogous.'[70] In *Stark Munro* he describes with a fond nostalgia his initial arrival in the town, when on his first night: 'I walked down to the Park, which is the chief centre of the place, and I found that I liked everything I saw of it. It was a lovely evening, and the air was fresh and sweet. I sat down and listened to the band for an hour, watching all the family parties.'[71] Southsea (the fictional Birchespool of the novel) is labelled 'the liveliest place I had ever seen',[72] 'really a delightful place',[73] and somewhere 'slowly, week by week, and month by month, the practice began to spread and to strengthen'.[74] As he wrote in one of his many letters to his mother at this time: '[Brother] Innes is very jolly and well and says Portsmouth is the best place ever he was in.'[75]

However, despite the rosy nostalgia of such writings, in reality it must have been taxing for the young doctor during the 'lonely and difficult'[76] first years as a GP: 'I shall sleep in my Ulster until you send down the blankets.'[77] He was mostly unimpressed by his own efforts at supplementing his income through fiction writing, dismissing them as 'feeble echoes of Bret Harte',[78] and in total during the first twelve months he lived at Bush Villas he earned a modest £156 2s 4d.[79] His notebook of the period shows him to have been so pessimistic about his future that he drafted an outline plan for a work poignantly titled 'The Autobiography of a Failure'.[80] Nevertheless, despite the hardships his resolution to succeed remained steadfast: 'There is nothing I put my mind to do that I have not done most completely.'[81] Perhaps in the most difficult moments he took comfort from the knowledge that he was then residing in a town with pronounced literary connections, being the birthplace of Dickens, Besant and Meredith, and the childhood home of Kipling. It was also, though he did not know it at the time, the current residence of H.G. Wells, who worked in Hyde's Drapers, in the King's Road part of the town.

Gradually, over time, the number of patients Doyle administered increased, and he remained ever open to opportunities he might exploit: 'There is a fine opening here, a great many medical men have died lately and the survivors are awful duffers.'[82] His efforts at supporting himself through his two-track career began to pay off, and by the end of his stay in Southsea he had written and published a varied range of works, with a back catalogue that included shorter fictions such as 'J. Habakuk Jephson's Statement', 'The Winning Shot', 'The Mystery of Sasassa Valley', 'The Captain of the *Polestar*', 'The fate of the *Evangeline*', 'Crabbe's Practice', 'Uncle Jeremy's Household', and 'Cyprian Overbeck Wells (A Literary Mosaic)', as well as novels such as *The Narrative of John Smith* (for years 'lost in the post in its initial submission to a publisher'[83] and only appearing again in a Christie's auction in 2004), *The Firm of Girdlestone*, and *Micah Clarke*. Indeed, what is impressive, as Daniel Stashower has pointed out, is that despite the challenges of setting up a practice in an unfamiliar town, with little support from others, Conan Doyle produced 'most of his memorable early work...dashing off a few lines in between patients or in the evening after the doors of the surgery had closed'.[84]

In addition to furthering his medical and writing careers, Doyle also became an enthusiastic resident of Portsmouth. He joined local sports clubs, including those for bowls and tennis, and was the local cricket club captain. It was also at this time, on Tuesday 14th October 1884, that 'Portsmouth Football Club' was established, under official Football Association rules. And thus it was no surprise that, come only the second official match of this team on Boxing Day of the same year, Arthur Conan Doyle could be found playing in goal – even if under the pseudonym A.C. Smith, a precaution taken owing to his concern that being publicly associated with a primarily working-class sport might damage his reputation as a professional medical man.[85] On 30th December 1886, that Portsmouth team, with Doyle playing outfield this time, beat the Royal Marines 10-0 and were lauded in the local *Portsmouth Times* for their labours: 'The full backs, particularly A.C. Smith, did what work devolved upon them so satisfactorily that the office of the Portsmouth goalkeeper was quite a sinecure.'[86] And on 26th March 1887, the team went as far as winning the Portsmouth & District Cup, with Doyle reprising his role as goalkeeper: 'At the party in the Blue Anchor afterwards the cup was presented by General Harward, Vice-President of the club. He made an appropriate speech mentioning many of the players by name, and...gave the game away by referring to Smith throughout as Doyle.'[87]

At a personal level, perhaps the most significant thing to happen to Arthur in Portsmouth was to meet his first wife, Louise. She was the sister of a meningitis patient he had unsuccessfully tended in 1885, and they were to marry and start their own family in the year following her brother's demise. But beyond such personal developments, Portsmouth was the site for the beginning of the two main strands of the rest of Conan Doyle's professional life. First, it was there that he attended his first séance, at Kingston Lodge on 24th January 1887,[88] then later that year a medium (16th June 1887), both of which precipitated a fundamental change in his belief system: '[this] marks in my spiritual career the change of "I believe" into "I know".'[89] In a letter to the spiritualist *Light* magazine about these experiences he stated unambiguously that 'after many months of enquiry'[90] he was now convinced that 'it was absolutely certain that intelligence could exist apart from the body'.[91] He had acknowledged the call of the Spiritualist cause, and went on to join the Society for Psychical Research and become Vice President of the Hampshire Psychical Society, and spend his later years fervently advocating the Spiritualist cause in the UK and overseas.

The second major development in Doyle's professional life whilst in Portsmouth was his evolution as a fiction writer, and obviously in particular his creation of Sherlock Holmes. From an original outline story featuring Sherrinford Holmes and Ormond Sacker titled 'A Tangled Skein', to the final published version featuring Sherlock Holmes and Dr John Watson in what was by then *A Study in Scarlet,* he harnessed all of his writing skills in manufacturing his own fictional detective, a contribution to the emerging genre of detective fiction initiated decades earlier by writers such as Edgar Allan Poe and Emile Gaboriau:

I felt now that I was capable of something fresher and crisper and more workmanlike. Gaboriau had rather attracted me by the neat dovetailing of his plots, and Poe's masterful detective, M. Dupin, had from boyhood been one of my heroes. But could I bring an addition of my own? I thought of my old teacher Joe Bell, of his eagle face, of his curious ways, of his eerie trick of spotting details. If he were a detective he would surely reduce this fascinating but unorganised business to something nearer to an exact science. I would try if I could get this effect. It was surely possible in real life, so why should I not make it plausible in fiction?

Despite its relatively short gestation period (he started writing *A Study in Scarlet* during the spring, 8th March of 1886, and had finished it by mid-April),[93] it was to be perhaps the most significant five weeks of his professional life, even though he did not see it as such as the time: 'Ward Lock made a wonderful bargain, for they not only had their Christmas number but they brought out numerous editions of the book, and finally they even had the valuable cinema rights for this paltry payment. I never at any time received another penny for it from this firm, so I do not feel that I need be grateful even if it so chanced that they cleared my path in life.'[94] It would see the creation of Holmes and initiate the worldwide legacy to follow, as well as giving focus and direction to his writing career and leading to other acclaimed non-Sherlockian works such as *Micah Clarke* (1889), which was also written in Southsea and ended up achieving significant sales 'approaching 10,000 copies'.[95]

All of this meant that within only a handful of years Conan Doyle became a noteworthy feature of the local cultural landscape. His achievements were celebrated energetically, as a review in the *Hampshire Post* of 2nd December 1887 makes clear: 'We know of no more brilliant example than the little story which Dr Doyle has just given to the world.'[96] Such a public profile meant that he was a necessary guest at all high-profile local functions, including a civic banquet for Walter Besant on 19th January 1888 at the Victoria Hall,[97] and the official opening of the new Guildhall on 7th August 1890, attended by the Prince of Wales.[98] Doyle had been taken to the heart of the town, and the local media never tired of drawing attention to his achievements: 'Dr Conan Doyle has gone at one stride into the front rank of novelists,' and finished with, 'We do not say this because Dr Conan Doyle is a resident of Portsmouth. A man's town is generally the last place to recognise his capacity.'[99]

Beyond this local celebrity, Conan Doyle was also starting to achieve a national and international reputation. This precipitated an invitation to dine in London with the American editor of *Lippincott's Magazine*, in the August of 1889. It is an evening at the Langham Hotel that is now part of the folklore of Sherlock Holmes. For, as Doyle himself later put it:

Now for the second time I was in London on literary business. Stoddart, the American, proved to be an excellent fellow, and had two others to dinner. They were Gill, a very entertaining Irish M.P., and Oscar Wilde, who was already famous as the champion of aestheticism. It was indeed a golden evening for me. Wilde to my surprise had read *Micah Clarke* and was enthusiastic about it, so that I did not feel a complete outsider. His conversation left an indelible impression upon my mind. He towered above us all, and yet had the art of seeming to be interested in all that we could say. He had delicacy of feeling and tact, for the monologue man, however clever, can never be a gentleman at heart. He took as well as gave, but what he gave was unique. He had a curious precision of statement, a delicate flavour of humour, and a trick of small gestures to illustrate his meaning, which were peculiar to himself...the result of the evening was that both Wilde and I promised to write books for *Lippincott's Magazine*—Wilde's contribution was *The Picture of Dorian Gray,* a book which is surely upon a high moral plane, while I wrote *The Sign of Four,* in which Holmes made his second appearance.[100]

Perhaps until this point, Doyle had started to believe that his growing personal and professional success and happiness could be maintained whilst living in Southsea. But during this evening at the Langham, in the company of global celebrity and artistic genius, it is likely that the allure of the Metropolis began to make its own appeal to him. Whatever the truth of the matter, in less than a year from the publication of *The Sign of Four* the Conan Doyle family had departed their south-coast home for good. On 24th November 1890, the young doctor and emerging writer 'gave an interview to the local *Evening News* announcing his intention to give up his practice and leave the town',[101] and by 12th December his friends had organised a leaving party at the Grosvenor Hotel – presided over by one Dr James Watson. Brother Innes (who was attending Portsmouth Grammar School in order to cram for his army exams), took lodgings with Alfred Wood, a mathematics master at the school and cricketing friend of Arthur, baby daughter Mary went to stay with her grandmother on the Isle of Wight, and the Conan Doyle family left Bush Villas: 'On a day late in December, 1890, a four-wheeler stood at the door. Their trunks were strapped to its roof. In Elm Grove, the snow was falling past curtainless windows. Once or twice he thought, as he handed Touie into the cab, how much he had tried here and how little he had succeeded in the world. But he put the thought aside, his arm round Touie, as the cab moved away into the snow.'[102]

The period 1882–1890 had been foundational for Arthur and his family; this is born out by the fact that he never lost his fondness for his old home. He returned as a visitor on several occasions, including the time the *Portsmouth Times* noted that 'Dr Conan Doyle...is staying in the town for six weeks after his trip to Egypt.'[103] In June 1896, he even bought property in Southsea, 53 Kent Road, renting it to his friend Dr Vernon Ford.[104] In his autobiography Conan Doyle offered his most heartfelt tribute to the place where the different elements of his personal and professional life started to come together in such a momentous fashion:

> With its imperial associations it is a glorious place and even now if I had to live in a town outside London it is surely to Southsea, the residential quarter of Portsmouth, that I would turn. The history of the past carries on into the history of today, the new torpedo-boat flies past the old Victory with the same white ensign flying from each, and the old Elizabethan culverins and sakers can still be seen in the same walk which brings you to the huge artillery of the forts. There is a great glamour there to any one with the historic sense – a sense which I drank in with my mother's milk.[105]

As he later acknowledged, if it had not been for the ambitious restlessness that began to creep up on him after that evening at the Langham Hotel, Conan Doyle might 'well have stayed in practice in Southsea for the rest of his life'.[106] And if he had, he told his mother, he would not have been disappointed.[107] But, as it turned out, a mixture of professional drive and the growing demands of being the creator and author of Sherlock Holmes drew him away to London; the place to which, as he noted himself, all the loungers and idlers of the Empire were irresistibly drained.

Neil McCaw
Southsea, 2017

Notes

1   *The Adventures of Sherlock Holmes* (1892); *The Memoirs of Sherlock Holmes* (1894); *The Return of Sherlock Holmes* (1905).

2   Colin Dexter, 'Introduction' to Sir Arthur Conan Doyle, *The Adventure of the Lion's Mane*, a facsimile of the original Sherlock Holmes Manuscript with an Introduction by Colin Dexter and Afterword by Richard Lancelyn Green (London: Westminster Libraries The Sherlock Holmes Society of London, 1992), p. 7

3   Barry Forshaw, 'The curious case of the author who would not die', *The Independent: Culture, Sunday March* 1st 2009; see http://www.independent.co.uk/arts-entertainment/books/features/the-curious-case-of-the-author-who-would-not-die-1634753.html. Accessed 23rd December 2016.

4   Sir Arthur Conan Doyle, 'The Adventure of the Creeping Man' in *The Case-Book of Sherlock Holmes,* with an introduction by W. W. Robson (Oxford: Oxford University Press, 1993), p. 56'

5   Conan Doyle, 'The Adventure of the Creeping Man,' p. 50

6   D. Martin Dakin, *A Sherlock Holmes Commentary* (London: David & Charles, 1972), p. 249

7   Dakin, p. 249

8   W.W. Robson, 'Introduction' to *The Case-Book of Sherlock Holmes,* p. xviii

9   Robson, 'Introduction', p. xviii

10 Nicholas Meyer, *The Seven Per Cent Solution* (London: Companion, 1976), p. 19

11 Meyer, p. 19

12 David Stuart Davies, 'Afterword' to Sir Arthur Conan Doyle, *The Case-Book of Sherlock Holmes,* Collector's Library (New York: Barnes & Noble, 2004), pp. 295-302 (295)

13 Stuart Davies, 'Afterword', p. 295

14 Stuart Davies, 'Afterword', p. 297

15 Michael Hardwick, *The Complete Guide to Sherlock Holmes* (New York: St Martin's, 1986), p. 184

16 Hardwick, p. 185

17 Hardwick, p. 189

18 Sir Arthur Conan Doyle, *Memories and Adventures* (London: Wordsworth, 2007), p. 84

19 Conan Doyle, *Memories and Adventures,* p. 84

20 Stuart Davies, 'Afterword', p. 297

21 Sir Arthur Conan Doyle, 'The Adventure of the Cardboard Box'; see http://www.gutenberg.org/files/2344/2344-h/2344-h.htm. Accessed 29th December 2016.

22 Stuart Davies, 'Afterword', p. 300

23 Robson, 'Introduction', p. xv

24 Robson, 'Introduction', p. xvii

25 Robson, 'Introduction', p. xvii

26 Vincent Starrett, '221b'; see, for example, https://allpoetry.com/poem/8599039-221b-by-Vincent-Starrett. Accessed 24th December 2016.

27 A range of Sherlockian scholars have explored the science of this particular story. These include (but are by no means limited to): Richard Brown, 'Rejuvenation Therapy: Historical Background to "The Creeping Man"', *Canadian Holmes,* Volume 9, Number 2, Winter 1985, pp. 9-15; Arthur L Levine, 'Lowenstein's Other Creeper', *Baker Street Journal,* Volume 6, Number 1 (Jan 1956), pp. 30-33; J.C. Prager and Albert Silverstein, 'Lowenstein of Prague: the most maligned man in the Canon', *Baker Street Journal,* Volume 23, Number 4 (Dec 1973), pp. 220-27; and Charles A. Meyer's 'The Rehabilitation of "The Creeping Man"', *Baker Street Miscellanea,* 69 (Spring 1992), pp. 23-26 & 'The Real Creeps in "The Adventure of the Creeping Man"', *Naval Signals,* 30 (March 1993), pp. 3-8.

28 Leslie S. Klinger, 'The Adventure of the Creeping Man', in Leslie S. Klinger (ed.), *The New Annotated Sherlock Holmes,* Volume 2 (New York: W. W. Norton & Co., 2005), p. 1636

29 Stuart Davies, 'Afterword', p. 198

30 Conan Doyle, 'The Adventure of the Creeping Man', p. 67

31 The view that uncritically sees the contemporary world as at the summit of human knowledge and achievement, and which thus anachronistically misjudges or misreads the complexities and advances of the past.

32 H. G. Wells, *The Island of Dr Moreau* (Project Gutenberg, 2004) Chapter XV; see http://www.gutenberg.org/files/159/159-h/159-h.htm#ch15. Accessed 24th December 2016.

33 Charles Darwin, 'Introduction' to *On the Origin of Species* (1859) (Project Gutenberg, 2009); see http://www.gutenberg.org/files/1228/1228-h/1228-h.htm. Accessed 24th December 2016.

34 Max Nordau, *Degeneration* (London: William Heinemann, 1892), p. 2

Notes

35 Quoted in Nicole L. Miller and Brant R. Fulmer, 'Injection, Ligation and Transplantation: the Search for the Glandular Fountain of Youth', *The Journal of Urology,* Volume 177, June 2007, pp. 2000-2005 (2000)

36 Quoted in Miller and Fulmer, p. 2000

37 Dr Serge Voronoff, *Life: a study of the means of restoring vital energy and prolonging life,* translated by Evelyn Bostwick Voronoff (New York: E.P. Dutton & Co., 1920), p. 2

38 Voronoff, *Life,* p. 11

39 See Voronoff, 'Gland grafting would make us giants', *The Sunday Morning Star,* 19th June 1927; see https://news.google.com/newspapers?nid=2293&dat=19270619&id=7Q0nAAAAIBAJ&sjid=1wIGAAAAIBAJ&pg=863,2224820&hl=en. Accessed 27th December 2016.

40 For a supposed illustration of the 'before' and 'after' this procedure, see https://commons.wikimedia.org/wiki/File:%C3%89tude_sur_la_vieillesse_et_la_rajeunissement_par_la_greffe_Wellcome_L0068505.jpg. Accessed 27th December 2016.

41 See 'Hopes to find the fountain of youth in a monkey colony', *Lewiston Evening Journal,* 18th July 1923 at https://news.google.com/newspapers?nid=1913&dat=19230718&id=z3QpAAAAIBAJ&sjid=hWYFAAAAIBAJ&pg=2932,1194005&hl=en. Accessed 27th December 2016.

42 From the *Toledo Blade,* 30th August 1923; see https://news.google.com/newspapers?nid=1350&dat=19230830&id=aGJOAAAAIBAJ&sjid=Wf8DAAAAIBAJ&pg=2521,5901136&hl=en. Accessed 27th December 2016.

43 From *The Sunday Morning Star,* 1st July 1928; see https://news.google.com/newspapers?nid=2293&dat=19280701&id=_v0mAAAAIBAJ&sjid=swIGAAAAIBAJ&pg=973,5521666&hl=en. Accessed 27th December 2016.

44 From *The Pittsburgh Express,* 30th November 1930; see https://news.google.com/newspapers?nid=1144&dat=19301130&id=XkwbAAAAIBAJ&sjid=cEsEAAAAIBAJ&pg=4333,2400777&hl=en. Accessed 27th December 2016.

45 For instance, Voronoff's celebrity/infamy in Brazil is examined in Ethel Mizrahy Cuperschmid, 'Dr Voronoff's curious glandular xenoimplants', *História, Ciências, Saúde-Manguinhos,* Volume 14, Number 3, July-September 2007; see http://www.scielo.br/scielo.php?pid=S0104-59702007000300004&script=sci_arttext&tlng=en. Accessed 27th December 2016.

46 See, for instance, Henry T. Russell, 'Dr Voronoff foresees lengthening of life', *The Pittsburgh Express,* 21st October 1930; https://news.google.com/newspapers?nid=1144&dat=19301021&id=_kIdAAAAIBAJ&sjid=PUsEAAAAIBAJ&pg=2369,5752146&hl=en. Accessed 27th December 2016. Also, Kingsbury Smith, 'Voronoff, gland specialist, says normal life-span 140 years', *The Deseret News,* 14th January 1931; https://news.google.com/newspapers?nid=336&dat=19310114&id=seY0AAAAIBAJ&sjid=07UDAAAAIBAJ&pg=6866,1450862&hl=en. Accessed 27th December 2016.

47 Meyer, 1992, p. 24

48 Eric Grundhauser, 'The true story of Dr Voronoff's plan to use monkey testicles to make us immortal,' *Atlas Obscura,* 13th October 2015; see http://www.atlasobscura.com/articles/the-true-story-of-dr-voronoffs-plan-to-use-monkey-testicles-to-make-us-immortal. Accessed 27th December 2016.

49 Conan Doyle, 'The Adventure of the Creeping Man', p. 70

50 Conan Doyle, 'The Adventure of the Creeping Man', p. 70

51 Conan Doyle, 'The Adventure of the Creeping Man', p. 70

52 Walter Benjamin, 'The Work of Art in the Age of Mechanical Reproduction' in Hannah Arendt (ed.), *Illuminations,* translated by Harry Zohn (New York: Schokhen Books, 1969), p. 4

53 John Bryant, 'Witness and Access: the uses of the fluid text', *Textual Cultures: Texts, Contexts, Interpretation,* Volume 2, Number 1, Spring 2007, pp. 16-42 (17)

54 Bryant, 'Witness and Access', p. 17

55 Bryant, 'Witness and Access', p. 17

56 This was an extended version of Baring-Gould's chronology published in *The Baker Street Journal,* Volume 3, Number 1, pp. 238-51.

57 See, for just one of many examples, Andrew J. Peck and Leslie S. Klinger, *The Date Being..? A Compendium of Chronological Data* (New York: Magico Press, 1996).

58 Jerome McGann, *The Textual Condition* (New Jersey: Princeton University Press, 1991), p. 62

59 James L. W. West III, 'Are Manuscript Facsimiles Still Viable?' *Textual Cultures: Texts, Contexts, Interpretation,* Volume 6, Number 2, Spring 2001, pp. 103-108 (103)
60 Bryant, 'Witness and Access', p. 24
61 Richard's life and his fascination with Sherlock Holmes is discussed in more detail in the BBC documentary *The Man Who Loved Sherlock Holmes* (2007).
62 Arthur Conan Doyle, 'To Mary Doyle, Southsea - June 1882' in Jon Lellenberg, Daniel Stashower & Charles Foley (eds), *Arthur Conan Doyle: A Life in Letters* (London: HarperPress, 2007), p. 160
63 John Dickson Carr, *The Life of Sir Arthur Conan Doyle* (New York: Carroll & Graf, 2003), p. 22
64 Geoffrey Stavert, *A Study in Southsea* (Portsmouth: Milestone, 1987), p. 14
65 Andrew Lycett, *Conan Doyle: the Man who Created Sherlock Holmes* (London: Weidenfeld & Nicolson, 2007), P. 87
66 Conan Doyle, *Memories and Adventures,* p. 54
67 Andrew Lycett, p. 85
68 Arthur Conan Doyle, 'To Mary Doyle, Southsea - June 1882' in Lellenberg, Stashower & Foley (eds), p. 162
69 Sir Arthur Conan Doyle, *The Stark Munro Letters* (Newcastle: Cambridge Scholars Press, 2008), p. 90
70 Conan Doyle, *Memories and Adventures,* p. 52
71 Conan Doyle, *The Stark Munro Letters,* p. 97
72 Conan Doyle, *The Stark Munro Letters,* p. 98
73 Conan Doyle, *The Stark Munro Letters,* p. 101
74 Conan Doyle, *The Stark Munro Letters,* p. 140
75 ACD to Mary Doyle, July 1882, Folio 44, British Library Archive Add MS 88924/1/5
76 Andrew Lycett, p. 87
77 ACD to Mary Doyle, June 1882, Folio 28, British Library Archive Add MS 88924/1/5
78 Conan Doyle, *Memories and Adventures,* p. 53
79 Lycett, p. 93
80 Lycett, p. 108
81 ACD to Mary Doyle, June 1882, Folio 30, British Library Archive Add MS 88924/1/5
82 ACD to Mary Doyle, June 1882, Folio 33, British Library Archive Add MS 88924/1/5
83 Russell Miller, *The Adventures of Arthur Conan Doyle* (London: Pimlico, 2009), p. 99
84 Daniel Stashower, *Teller of Tales: the Life of Arthur Conan Doyle* (New York: Henry Holt, 1999), p. 70
85 Stavert, p. 58
86 Stavert, p. 71
87 Stavert, p. 103
88 Lycett, p. 124
89 Lycett, p. 130
90 Lycett, p. 130
91 Lycett, p. 131
92 Conan Doyle, *Memories and Adventures,* p. 62
93 Lycett, p. 118
94 Conan Doyle, *Memories and Adventures,* p. 63
95 Lycett, p. 154
96 Stavert, p. 118
97 Stavert, p. 121
98 Stavert, p. 166
99 This review of *Micah Clarke* featured in the *Evening News* (25th February 1889); see Stavert, p. 138
100 Conan Doyle, *Memories and Adventures,* p. 66
101 Lycett, p. 157
102 Dickson Carr, p. 62
103 The article was published Saturday 16th May 1896; see Stavert, p. 173
104 Stavert, p. 184
105 Conan Doyle, *Memories and Adventures,* p. 55
106 Miller, p. 127
107 ACD to Mary Doyle, 20th November 1888, Folio 20, British Library Archive Add MS 88924/1/7

Works Cited

Sir Arthur Conan Doyle, *The Stark Munro Letters* (Newcastle: Cambridge Scholars Press, 2008)

Sir Arthur Conan Doyle, *The Case-Book of Sherlock Holmes,* with an introduction by W. W. Robson (Oxford: Oxford University Press, 1993)

Sir Arthur Conan Doyle, *The Adventure of the Lion's Mane*, a facsimile of the original Sherlock Holmes Manuscript with an Introduction by Colin Dexter and Afterword by Richard Lancelyn Green (London: Westminster Libraries The Sherlock Holmes Society of London, 1992)

Sir Arthur Conan Doyle, *Memories and Adventures* (London: Wordsworth, 2007)

Sir Arthur Conan Doyle, 'The Adventure of the Cardboard Box'; see http://www.gutenberg.org/files/2344/2344-h/2344-h.htm

ACD to Mary Doyle, July 1882, Folio 44, British Library Archive Add MS 88924/1/5

ACD to Mary Doyle, June 1882, Folio 28, British Library Archive Add MS 88924/1/5

ACD to Mary Doyle, June 1882, Folio 30, British Library Archive Add MS 88924/1/5

ACD to Mary Doyle, June 1882, Folio 33, British Library Archive Add MS 88924/1/5

ACD to Mary Doyle, 20th November 1888, Folio 20, British Library Archive Add MS 88924/1/7

Hannah Arendt (ed.), *Illuminations,* translated by Harry Zohn (New York: Schokhen Books, 1969)

George Bornstein, *Material Modernism: The Politics of the Page* (New York: Cambridge University Press, 2001)

John Bryant, 'Witness and Access: the uses of the fluid text', *Textual Cultures: Texts, Contexts, Interpretation,* Volume 2, Number 1, spring 2007, pp. 16-42

John Dickson Carr, *The Life of Sir Arthur Conan Doyle* (New York: Carroll & Graf, 2003)

Roger Chartier, 'Laborers and Voyagers: from the text to the reader', *Diacritics,* 22:2, summer 1992, pp. 49-61

Ethel Mizrahy Cuperschmid, 'Dr Voronoff's curious glandular xenoimplants', *História, Ciências, Saúde-Manguinhos,* Volume 14, Number 3, July-September 2007; see http://www.scielo.br/scielo.php?pid=S0104-59702007000300004&script=sci_arttext&tlng=en

D. Martin Dakin, *A Sherlock Holmes Commentary* (London: David & Charles, 1972)

Charles Darwin, 'Introduction' to *On the Origin of Species* (1859) (Project Gutenberg, 2009); see http://www.gutenberg.org/files/1228/1228-h/1228-h.htm

Sir Arthur Conan Doyle, *The Case-Book of Sherlock Holmes,* edited by David Stuart Davies, Collector's Library (New York: Barnes & Noble, 2004)

Barry Forshaw, 'The curious case of the author who would not die', *The Independent: Culture,* Sunday March 1st 2009

Eric Grundhauser, 'The true story of Dr Voronoff's plan to use monkey testicles to make us immortal', *Atlas Obscura,* 13th October 2015

Michael Hardwick, *The Complete Guide to Sherlock Holmes* (New York: St Martin's, 1986)

Leslie S. Klinger (ed.), *The New Annotated Sherlock Holmes,* Volume 2 (New York: W. W. Norton & Co., 2005)

Jon Lellenberg, Daniel Stashower & Charles Foley, *Arthur Conan Doyle: A Life in Letters* (London: HarperPress, 2007)

Andrew Lycett, *Conan Doyle: the Man who Created Sherlock Holmes* (London: Weidenfeld & Nicolson, 2007)

Jerome McGann, *The Textual Condition* (New Jersey: Princeton University Press, 1991)

Charles A. Meyer's 'The Rehabilitation of "The Creeping Man"', *Baker Street Miscellanea,* 69 (Spring 1992), pp. 23-26

Nicholas Meyer, *The Seven Per Cent Solution* (London: Companion, 1976)

Nicole L. Miller and Brant R. Fulmer, 'Injection, Ligation and Transplantation: the Search for the Glandular Fountain of Youth', *The Journal of Urology,* Volume 177, June 2007, pp. 2000-2005

Russell Miller, *The Adventures of Arthur Conan Doyle* (London: Pimlico, 2009)

Max Nordau, *Degeneration* (London: William Heinemann, 1892)

Andrew J. Peck and Leslie S. Klinger, *The Date Being..? A Compendium of Chronological Data* (New York: Magico Press, 1996)

Meg Roland, 'Facsimile Editions: Gesture and Projection', *Textual Cultures: Texts, Contexts, Interpretation,* Volume 6, Number 2, 2011, pp. 48-59

Vincent Starrett, '221b'; see https://allpoetry.com/poem/8599039-221b-by-Vincent-Starrett

Daniel Stashower, *Teller of Tales: the Life of Arthur Conan Doyle* (New York: Henry Holt, 1999)

Geoffrey Stavert, *A Study in Southsea* (Portsmouth: Milestone, 1987)

Dr Serge Voronoff,
    Life: a study of the means of restoring vital energy and prolonging life, translated by
    Evelyn Bostwick Voronoff (New York: E.P. Dutton & Co., 1920)
    'Gland grafting would make us giants', *The Sunday Morning Star,* 19th June 1927

H. G. Wells, *The Island of Dr Moreau* (Project Gutenberg, 2004) Chapter XV

James L. W. West III, 'Are Manuscript Facsimiles Still Viable?' *Textual Cultures: Texts, Contexts, Interpretation,* Volume 6, Number 2, spring 2001, pp. 103-108

The Adventure
of the Creeping Man

An annotated transcription of Conan Doyle's
original handwritten story

THE
ADVENTURE
OF THE
CREEPING MAN

A Sherlock Holmes Story

*M*r Sherlock Holmes was always of opinion that I should publish the singular facts connected with Professor Presbury, if only to dispel once for all the ugly rumours which some twenty years ago[1] agitated the University and were echoed in the learned societies of London. There were however certain obstacles in the way, and the true history of this curious case remained entombed in the tin box which contains so many records of my friend's adventures. Now we have at last obtained permission to ventilate the facts which formed one of the very last cases handled by Holmes before his retirement from practise. Even now a certain reticence and discretion have to be observed in laying the matter before the public.

It was one Sunday evening early in September of the year 1902[2] that I received one of Holmes' laconic messages, "come at one if convenient – if inconvenient come all the same. S.H."[3] The relations between us in those latter days were peculiar. He was a man of habits, narrow and concentrated habits, and I

---

1   The story was first published in March 1923 in both *The Strand Magazine* (with illustrations by Howard K. Elcock) and *Hearst's International Magazine* (previously *The World Today,* and later to be absorbed by *Cosmopolitan* – with illustrations by Frederic Dorr Steele). Watson's confession that he is writing his version of the events 'nearly two decades' after they took place in 1902, thus places him in the earlier years of the 1920s.

2   In the 'Introduction' to this volume I analyze in detail the significance of the fact that in all other versions of the story this date has been revised to 1903, which establishes the position of 'The Creeping Man' towards the end of the chronology of the Holmes stories, and the last story before his retirement. In terms of the 'real-world' history of the story, whether it is dated as 1902 or 1903 this still identifies 'The Creeping Man' as one of the Edwardian rather than Victorian Sherlock Holmes tales, with Queen Victoria having died in January 1901.

3   This is one of the most well-known examples of Holmes's pithiness, and as such is a perfect rebuttal to those critics who have called into question the quality of Conan Doyle's writing within the story.

The Adventure of the Creeping Man

Mr Sherlock Holmes was always of opinion that I should publish the singular facts connected with Professor Presbury, if only to dispel once for all the ugly rumours which some twenty years ago agitated the University and were echoed in the learned societies of London. There were however certain obstacles in the way, and the true history of this curious case remained entombed in the tin box which contains so many records of my friend's adventures. Now we have at last obtained ~~Presbury's~~ permission to ventilate the facts which formed one of the very last cases handled by ~~way~~ Holmes before his retirement from practise. Even now a certain reticence and discretion have to be observed in laying the matter before the public.

It was one sunday evening early in September of the year 1902 that I received one of Holmes' laconic messages, "Come at once if convenient — if inconvenient come all the same. S. H". The relations between us in those latter days were peculiar. He was a man of habits, narrow & concentrated habits, and I had become one of them. As an institution I was like the violin, the shag tobacco, the old black pipe,[4] the index books, and others perhaps less excusable. When it was a case of active work and a comrade was needed upon whose nerve he could place some reliance, my role was obvious. But apart from this I had uses. I was a whetstone for his mind. I stimulated him. He liked to think aloud in my presence. His remarks could hardly be said to be made to me – many of them would have been as appropriately addressed to his bedstead – but none the less, having formed the habit it had become in some way helpful that I should register and interject. If I irritated him by a certain methodical slowness in my mentality, that irritation served only to make his own flame-like intuitions and impressions flash up the more vividly and swiftly. Such was my humble role in our alliance.

When I arrived at Baker Street[5] I found him huddled up in his armchair with updrawn knees,[6] his pipe in his mouth and his brow furrowed with thought. It was clear that he was in the throes of some vexatious problem. With a wave of his

---

4   Watson is self-consciously identifying himself as a familiar element of the Holmesian iconography. However, one of the very remarkable things about Sherlock Holmes is the way so many elements of the wider mythology are rooted not in the Conan Doyle stories, but rather the vast number of film, television and stage adaptations of the Great Detective. See (for example) http://ed.ted.com/lessons/who-is-sherlock-holmes-neil-mccaw

5   This obviously identifies the story as taking place during a period when Holmes and Watson are not living together at Baker Street.

6   There is an interesting self-reflexivity to how Conan Doyle echoes his own earlier descriptions of Holmes, such in 'The Red-Headed League' (1891) – 'He curled himself up in his chair, with his thin knees drawn up to his hawk-like nose, and there he sat with his eyes closed and his black clay pipe thrusting out like the bill of some strange bird.' See http://www.victorianweb.org/art/illustration/pagets/16.html

had become one of them. I was like the violin, the shag tobacco, the old black pipe, the index books, and others perhaps less excusable. When it was a case of active work and a comrade was needed upon whose nerve he could place some reliance, my role was obvious. But apart from this I had uses. I was a whetstone for his mind. I stimulated him. He liked to think aloud in my presence. His remarks could hardly be said to be made to me — many of them would have been as appropriately addressed to his bedstead — but none the less, having formed the habit it had become in some way helpful that I should register and interject. If I irritated him by a certain methodical slowness in my mentality, that irritation served only to make his own flame-like intuitions and impressions flash up the more vividly and swiftly. Such was my humble role in our alliance.

When I arrived at Baker Street I found him huddled up in his armchair with updrawn knees, his pipe in his mouth and his brow furrowed with thought. It was clear that he was in the throes of some vexatious problem. With a wave of his hand he indicated my old arm chair, but otherwise for half an hour he gave no sign that he was aware of my presence. Then with a start he seemed to come from his reverie, and with his usual whimsical smile, he greeted me back to what had once been my home.

"You will excuse a certain abstraction of mind, my Dear Watson" said he "some curious facts have been submitted to me within the last 24 hours, and they in turn have given rise to some speculations of a more general character. I have serious thoughts of writing a small monograph upon the uses of dogs in the work of the detective[7]"

"But surely, Holmes, this has been explored" said I "Blood hounds – sleuth hounds –"

"No, no Watson, that side of the matter is of course obvious. But there is another which is far more subtle. You may recollect that in the case which you, in your sensational way, coupled with the Copper Beeches,[8] I was able by watching the mind of the child to form a deduction as to the criminal habits of the very smug and respectable father"

7   There have been numerous pieces of Sherlockian scholarship that have considered the significance of dogs within the Canon. These include (as discussed in the 'Introduction') Emma Mason's 'Dogs, detectives and the famous Sherlock Holmes.'

8   'The Adventure of the Copper Beeches' was first published in *The Strand Magazine* in June 1892. It is the last of the twelve stories of *The Adventures of Sherlock Holmes.*

hand he indicated my old arm chair, but otherwise for half
an hour he gave no sign that he was aware of my presence.
Then with a start he seemed to come ~~and~~ from his reverie, and
with his usual ~~abstract~~ whimsical. smile, he greeted me back to what had
once been my home.

"You will excuse a certain abstraction of mind, my
dear Watson" said he "Some curious facts have been submitted
to me within the last 24 hours, and they in turn have given rise
to some speculations of a more general character. I have serious
thoughts of writing ~~some~~ a small monograph upon the uses of dogs
in the work of the detective"

"But surely, Holmes, this has been explored" said I
"Blood hounds - sleuth hounds —"

"No, no, Watson, that side of the matter is ofcourse
obvious. But there is another which is far more subtle. You may
recollect that in the case which you, in your sensational way,
coupled with the Copper Beeches, I was able by watching the
mind of the child to form a deduction as to the criminal habits
of the very snug and respectable father"

"Yes, I remember it well"

"My line of thought about dogs is analogous. A dog reflects the family life. Who ever saw a frisky dog in a gloomy family, or a sad dog in a happy one? Snarling people have snarling dogs, dangerous people have dangerous ones.[9] And their passing moods may reflect the passing moods of others"

I shook my head. '"Surely, Holmes, this is a little farfetched" said I.

He had refilled his pipe and resumed his seat, taking no notice of my comment.

"The practical application of what I have said is very close to the problem I am investigating. It is a tangled skein,[10] you understand, and I am looking for a loose end. One possible loose end lies in the question why does Professor Presbury's faithful wolf hound **[Revised from 'spaniel'[11]]** Roy endeavour to bite him."

I sank back in my chair in some disappointment. Was it for so trivial a question as this that I had been summoned from my work! Holmes glanced across at me.

"The same old Watson" said he "you never learn

---

9   This is typical of the kind of generalisations about human traits and behaviours on which Holmes's famous powers of 'deduction' are based. They are a necessary feature of the wider pretence that *deduction* (knowledge ascertained through logical inevitability) is central to the Holmesian method. Whereas, as has been noted by various others, in truth Holmes's methods are more induction (linked to the probability of outcomes) than deduction.

10 'The Tangled Skein' (thread, or yarn) was the working title of the first Holmes novel, *A Study in Scarlet* (1887).

11 As discussed at greater length in the 'Introduction,' Conan Doyle's initial version of 'Roy' saw him as a 'faithful spaniel.' Bearing in mind the author's evident fondness for fierce dogs as Gothic fictional centerpieces (*The Hound of the Baskervilles*, 'The Copper Beeches' etc.) it would seem likely that the shift from spaniel to wolfhound was at least in part motivated by a desire to ramp up the eventual melodrama of the conclusion to 'The Creeping Man.'

" Yes, I remember it well "

" My line of thoughts about dogs is analogous. A dog reflects the family life. Who ever saw a frisky dog in a gloomy family, or a sad dog in a happy one? Snarling people have snarling dogs, dangerous people have dangerous ones. And their passing moods may reflect the passing moods of others"

I shook my head. " Surely, Holmes, this is a little far fetched " said I.

He had refilled his pipe and resumed his seat, taking no notice of my comment.

" The practical application of what I have said is very close to the problem which I am investigating. It is a tangled skein, you understand, and I am looking for a loose end. ~~what meant~~ One possible loose end lies in the question why does Professor Presbury's faithful ~~spaniel~~ wolf hound Roy endeavours to bite him".

I sank back in my chair in some disappointment. Was it for so trivial a question as this that I had been summoned from my work? Holmes glanced across at me.

" The same old Watson " said he " you never learn

that the gravest issues may depend upon the smallest things. But is it not on the face of it strange that a staid elderly **[Revised from 'gentle learned old'[12]]** philosopher – you've heard of Presbury of course, the famous Camford[13] Physiologist? – that such a man whose friend has been his devoted wolf-hound **[Revised from 'spaniel'[14]]**, should now have been twice attacked by his own dog. What do you make of it?"

"The dog is ill"

"Well, that has to be considered. But he attacks no one else, nor does he apparently molest his master, save on very special occasions. Curious, Watson – very curious. But young Mr Bennett is **[Revised from 'overdue'[15]]** before his time if that is his ring. I had hoped to have a longer chat with you before he came"

There was a quick step on the stairs, a sharp tap at the door, and a moment later the new client presented himself. He was a tall handsome youth about thirty, well-dressed and elegant, but with something in his bearing which suggested the shyness of the student rather than the self-possession of the man of the world. He shook hands with Holmes, and then looked with some surprise at me.

---

12 This revision may be a matter solely of concision – there is no major substantive difference in the change in adjectives used to describe the Professor.

13 Much has been written within the context of what Sherlockians call 'the Game' (the willing suspension of disbelief within which all events and characters featured in the Holmes stories are seen as true) about Holmes's university days, and whether in this particular case 'Camford' represents Oxford University or Cambridge University. See (for example) N.P. Metcalfe, 'Oxford or Cambridge or Both?', or Nick Utechin, *Sherlock Holmes at Oxford*. Outside 'the Game' it is most likely that Conan Doyle, as a canny, audience-savvy writer and thinker, deliberately resisted any definitive correlation between Camford and either Oxford or Cambridge, in a desire not to alienate any readers (and alumni of either), and to secure him the artistic freedom of not having to depict the precise details of any one given (well-known) location.

14 See footnote 11

15 This is a relatively minor chronological change, but one that was necessary so that the following sentence made sense (assuming that the latter was written before the revision).

that the gravest issues may depend upon the smallest things. But is it not on the face of it strange that a staid elderly learned old philosopher — you've heard of Presbury of course, the famous Camford Physiologist? — that such a man whose own friend has been his devoted wolf-hound spaniel, should now have been twice attacked by his own dog. What do you make of it?"

"The dog is ill"

"Well, that has to be considered. But he attacks no one else, nor does he apparently molest his master, save on very special occasions. Curious, Watson - very curious. But young Mr. Bennett is before his time &. overdue Possibly that is his ring. I had hoped to have a longer chat with you before he came"

There was a quick step on the stair, a sharp tap at the door, and a moment later the new client presented himself. He was a tall handsome youth about thirty, well-dressed and elegant, but with something in his bearing which suggested the shyness of the student rather than the selfpossession of the man of the world. He shook hands with Holmes, and then looked with some surprise at me.

"This matter is very delicate, Mr Holmes" he said "Consider the relation in which I stand to Professor Presbury, both privately and publicly. I really can hardly justify myself if I speak before any third person"

"Have no fear, Mr Bennett. Dr Watson is the very soul of discretion and I can assure you that this is a matter in which I am very likely to need an assistant"

"As you like, Mr Holmes. You will, I am sure, understand my having some reserves in the matter."

"You will appreciate it, Watson, when I tell you that this gentleman, Mr Trevor Bennett, is professional assistant to the great scientist, lives under his roof, and is engaged to his only daughter.[16] Certainly we must agree that this Professor has every claim upon his loyalty and devotion. But it may best be shown by taking the necessary steps to clean up this strange mystery"

"I hope so, Mr Holmes. That is my one object. Does Dr Watson know the situation?"

"I have not had time to explain it"

---

16 This is yet another example of the father-daughter-suitor dramatic triangle that Conan Doyle was particularly fond of exploring, evident in previous tales including 'A Case of Identity' and 'The Copper Beeches.' It is a plot archetype particularly associated with Victorian and pre-Victorian literature, which was written at a time when the legal position of women was notably inferior to that of men. Until the 1857 Divorce and Matrimonial Causes Act in the United Kingdom, women's lives were often almost entirely under the legal control of their fathers or guardians, and husbands.

"This matter is very delicate, Mr Holmes" he said "Consider the relation in which I stand to Professor Presbury, both privately and publicly. I really can hardly justify myself if I speak before any third person"

"Have no fear, Mr Bennett. Dr Watson is the very soul of discretion and I can assure you that this is a matter in which I am very likely to need an assistant"

"As you like, Mr Holmes. You will, I am sure, understand my having some reserves in the matter."

"Dr Watson ~~will appreciate it~~ You will appreciate it, when I tell ~~him~~ You that this gentleman, Mr Trevor Bennett, is professional assistant to the great Scientist, lives under his roof, and is engaged to his ~~~~ only daughter. Certainly we must agree that the Professor has every claim upon ~~your~~ his loyalty & devotion. But it may best be shown by taking the necessary steps to clear up this strange mystery"

"I hope so, Mr Holmes. That is my one object. Does Dr Watson know the situation?."

"I have not had time to explain it"

"Then perhaps I had better go over the ground again before explaining some fresh developments"

"I will do so myself" said Holmes "in order to show that I have the events in their due order. The Professor, Watson, is a man of European reputation. His life has been academic. There has never been a breath of scandal **[Deletion of 'high duties nobly carved out made up his splendid record.'[17]]** He is a widower with one daughter, Edith. He is, I gather, a man of very virile and positive, one might almost say combative, character. So the matter stood until a very few months ago.

Then the current of his life was broken. He is sixty one years of age, but he became engaged to the daughter of Professor Morphy, his colleague in the chair of Comparative Anatomy.[18] It was not, as I understand, the reasoned courting of an elderly man, but rather the passionate frenzy of youth, for no one could have shown himself a more devoted lover. The lady, Alice Morphy was a very perfect girl both in mind and body, so that there was every excuse for the Professor's infatuation. None the less it did not meet full approval in his own family"

"We thought it rather excessive" said our

17   The switch to an active from a passive sentence in the revised version is more direct and concise. However, this does result in the regretful loss of the elegant description of the Professor that is present in the original manuscript.

18   Many scholars, including (but by no means limited to) N. P. Metcalfe (see above) and Jonathan McCafferty ('Will the Creeping Man Stand Up?'), have speculated both about the real-life model for Professor Presbury, and also the precise academic disciplinary specialism that Conan Doyle is alluding to in this story. It is perhaps equally likely that this is a further example of the relatively relaxed attitude Doyle displayed towards the factual accuracy of some of his Holmesian plot details.

" Then perhaps I had better go over the ground again before explaining some fresh developments."

" I will do so myself " said Holmes " in order to show that I have the events in their due order. The Professor, Watson, is a man of European reputation. His life has been academic. There has never been a breath of scandal. He is a widower with one daughter, Edith. He is, I gather, a man of very virile & positive, one might almost say combative, character. Duties nobly carried out make up his splendid record. So the matter stood until a very few months ago.

Then the current of his life was broken. He is sixty one years of age, but he became engaged to the daughter of Professor Morphy, his colleague in the chair of Comparative Anatomy. It was not, as I understand, the reasoned courting of an elderly man, but rather the passionate frenzy of youth, for no one could have shown himself a more devoted lover. The lady, Alice Morphy, was a very perfect girl both in mind and body, so that there was every excuse for the Professor's infatuation. None the less it did not meet full approval in his own family."

" We thought it rather excessive " said our

visitor.

"Exactly. Excessive and a little violent and unnatural. Professor Presbury was rich however and there was no objection upon the part of the father. The daughter however had other views, and there were already several candidates for her hand, who if they were less eligible from a worldly point of view were at least more of an age. The girl seemed to like the Professor in spite of his eccentricities **[Revised from 'liked Presbury…deeply as a friend'[19]]**. It was only age which stood in the way.

About this time a little mystery suddenly clouded the normal routine **[Revised from 'serenity'[20]]** of the Professor's life. He did what he had never done before. He left home and gave no indication where he was going. He was away a fortnight, and returned looking rather travel worn **[Revised from 'white and haggard'[21]]**. He made no allusion to where he had been, although he was the frankest of men. It chanced however that our client here, Mr Bennett, received a letter from a fellow student in Prague **[Revised from Paris[22]]**, who said that he was glad to have seen Professor Presbury there, although he had not been able to talk to him.

---

19 Doyle's original version of this part of the story could be seen to imply that the Professor's feelings for the young woman went unrequited – she cared for him 'as a friend,' whereas he clearly desired her in a more overtly sexual fashion. By removing this phrase Presbury is less likely to be viewed as predatory, as an experienced man wishing to impose his desires on an innocent, uninterested subject. This achieves an added sense of poignancy through the desperation of an elderly man who is prepared to do anything, including jeopardizing his mental and physical health, in pursuit of the younger woman he loves.

20 On reflection perhaps Conan Doyle felt that 'serenity' did not quite capture the nature of the Professor's life; certainly it is not a term usually associated with the career of a high-profile international academic.

21 This is one of a number of instances where Conan Doyle appears to be wrestling with the challenge of effectively pacing his narrative, and so to incrementally build the drama. The initial description of the Professor as 'white and haggard' does rather ramp up the drama before very much has happened, and replacing it with 'travel worn' pulls back on the reigns a little, introducing the reader to the idea that this man is undergoing a significant change, while allowing them to speculate as to the nature of this rather than fully spelling it out for them.

22 There are numerous instances within the Holmes canon where foreign associations, such as the Indian experiences of Dr Grimesby Roylott in 'The Speckled Band,' the Australian early life of John Turner in 'The Boscombe Valley Mystery,' or the American back-story of Effie Munro in 'The Yellow Face,' provide a background for subsequent acts of criminality. It is a frequent feature that foreign-ness is equated with immorality in some fashion. In this instance, what is particularly interesting in Conan Doyle's revision of 'Paris' into 'Prague' is the *kind* of foreign-ness that he is signifying - clearly on reflection he felt that the French capital did not quite achieve the sense of dubious, Gothic strangeness that he was seeking as the origin of the rejuvenating monkey serum, whereas the capital of what was then Bohemia, with all its medieval remoteness, was much closer to what he was looking for.

visitor.

"Exactly. Excessive and a little ~~violent and~~ unnatural. Professor Presbury was rich however and there was no objection upon the part of the father. The daughter however had other views, and there were already several candidates for her hand, who if they were less eligible from a worldly point of view were atleast more of an age. The girl ~~liked~~ seemed to like the Professor in spite of his eccentricities. ~~respected him deeply as a friend~~. It was only age which stood in the way.

About this time a little mystery suddenly clouded the normal ~~serenity~~ routine of the Professor's life. He did what he had never done before. He left home and gave no indication where he was going. He was away a fortnight, and returned looking ~~white and haggard~~ rather travel worn. He made no allusion to where he had been, although he was usually the frankest of men. It chanced however that our client here, Mr Bennett, received a letter from a fellow student in ~~Lewis~~ Prague, who said that he was glad to have seen Professor Presbury there, although he had not been able to talk to him.

Only in this way did his own household learn where he had been.

Now comes the point. From that time onwards a curious change came over the Professor. He became furtive and sly. Those round him had always the feeling that he was not the **[Deletion of 'frank light-hearted'**[23]**]** man that they had known but that he was under some shadow which had darkened his higher qualities. His intellect was not affected. His lectures were as brilliant as ever. **[Deletion of 'His health had become remarkably robust.'**[24]**]** But always there was something new, something sinister and unexpected. His daughter who was devoted to him tried again and again to resume the old **[Revised from 'candid'**[25]**]** relations and to penetrate this mask which her father seemed to have put on – you, sir, as I understand, did the same – but all was in vain. And now, Mr Bennett, tell in your own words the incident of the letters **[Revised from 'box'**[26]**].**"

"You must understand, Dr Watson, that the Professor had no secrets from me. If I were his son or his younger brother I could not have more completely enjoyed his confidence. As his secretary I handled every paper which came to him, and I opened and subdivided his letters. Shortly after his return all this was

---

23 Perhaps Conan Doyle decided the idea that the Professor had ever been 'light-hearted' might have been too much of a stretch for his readers to accept.

24 There is no obvious reason (other than concision) for removing the sentence. That said, it is possible Doyle felt there was a danger he might represent the speculative science of the story in too positive a light – any treatment or procedure which promises patients 'remarkably robust' health might be seen as too tempting to resist. The fact that we now know high-profile figures of the time including Sigmund Freud and W. B. Yeats were themselves seduced by the promise of such scientific advances might see such a concern as justified.

25 'Candid' would have worked perfectly well; the revision to 'old' perhaps better reinforces the sense of developing contrast in the relations between father and daughter in the past and in the present.

26 This revision appears to be a matter of narrative clarity – removing the potential ambiguity of the reference to the 'box.'

Only in this way did his own household learn where he had been.

Now comes the point. From that time onwards a curious change came over the Professor. He became furtive and sly. Those round him had always the feeling that he was not the frank ~~high-hearted~~ man that they had known but that he was under some shadow which had darkened his higher qualities. His intellect was not affected. His lectures were as brilliant as ever. ~~His health had become remarkably robust.~~ But always there was something new, something sinister and unexpected. His daughter who was devoted to him tried again & again to resume the old ~~cordial~~ relations and to penetrate this mask which her father seemed to have put on — You, sir, as I understand, did the same — but all was in vain. And now, Mr. Bennett, tell in your own words the incident of the ~~box~~ letters."

"You must understand, Dr. Watson, that the Professor had no secrets from me. If I were his son or his younger brother I could not have more completely enjoyed his confidence. As his secretary I handled every paper which came to him, and I opened & subdivided his letters. Shortly after his return all this was changed. He told me that certain letters might come to him from London which would be marked by a cross under the stamp. This were to be set aside for his own **[Deletion of 'private'[27]]** eyes only. I may say that several of these did pass through my hands, that they had the EC[28] mark, and were in an illiterate[29] hand writing. If he answered them at all the answers did not pass through my hands nor into the letter basket in which all correspondence was collected."

"And the box" said Holmes.

"Ah yes, the box. The Professor brought back a little wooden box from his travels. It was the one thing which suggested a continental tour, for it was one of those quaint carved things which one associates with Germany.[30] This he placed in his instrument cupboard. One day in looking for a canula[31] I took up the box. To my surprise he was very angry and reproved me **[Deletion of 'warmly']** in words which were quite savage for my curiosity. It was the first time such a thing had happened and I was deeply hurt. I endeavoured to explain that it was a mere accident that I had touched the box, but all evening I was conscious that he looked at me harshly and that the incident was rankling in his mind."

27 The original 'own private eyes' is rather tautological.
28 This denotes the 'East Central' London postal mark, part of the wider postal convention (evident in various countries) whereby letters and parcels are stamped with their place of origin.
29 As has been noted by numerous others, this is an example of a Conan Doylean slip – a half-malapropism in which 'illiterate' has been written instead of 'illegible.'
30 As has already been noted, throughout the Sherlockian canon Conan Doyle represents variations of foreign-ness in loaded terms. Here, the association with Germany, alongside the previous allusion to Prague, reinforces the sense of Gothic otherness; this is a fundamental aspect of how Doyle represents the dubious scientific practices at the heart of the story.
31 This is misspelt in the original handwritten text.

changed. He told me that certain letters might come to him from London which would be marked by a cross under the stamp. These were to be set aside for his own eyes only. I may say that several of these did pass through my hands, that they had the EC mark, and were in an illiterate hand writing. If he answered them at all the answer did not pass through my hands nor into the letter basket in which our correspondence was collected."

"And the box" said Holmes.

"Ah yes, the box. The Professor brought back a little wooden box from his travels. It was the one thing which suggested a continental tour, for it was one of those quaint carved things which one associates with Germany. This he placed in his instrument cupboard. One day in looking for a canula I took up the box. To my surprise he was very angry and reproved me warmly in words which were quite savage for my curiosity. It was the first time such a thing had happened and I was deeply hurt. I endeavoured to explain that it was a mere accident that I had touched the box, but all evening I was conscious that he looked at me harshly and that the incident was rankling in his mind."

Mr Bennett drew a little diary book from his pocket "That was on the 2nd of July[32]" said he.

"You are certainly an admirable witness" said Holmes "I may need some of these dates which you have noted"

"I learned method among other things from my great teacher. From the time that I observed abnormality in his behaviour I felt that it was my duty to study his case. Thus I have it here that it was on that very day, July 2nd, that Roy attacked the Professor, as he came from his study into the hall. Again on July 11th there was a scene of the same sort, and then I have a note of yet another upon July 20th. After that we had to banish Roy to the stables. He was a dear affectionate animal – but I fear I weary you"

Mr Bennett spoke in a tone of reproach for it was very clear that Holmes was not listening. His face was rigid and his eyes gazed abstractedly at the ceiling. With an effort he recovered himself.

"Singular! Most singular!" he murmured. "These details were new to me, Mr Bennett. I think we have

---

32 Both W. S. Baring-Gould (*The Annotated Sherlock Holmes* (New York: Wing Books, 1967), p. 761) & Leslie S. Klinger (*The New Annotated Sherlock Holmes*, Volume 2 (New York: W. W. Norton & Co., 2005), p. 1665), offer detailed chronologies of the narrative of 'The Creeping Man.' Readers studying Conan Doyle's handwritten manuscript will notice evidence that he was also very concerned to map out the story accurately; it is equally apparent from various revisions and crossings-out that he found this task a significant challenge.

Mr Bennett drew a little diary book from his pocket "That was on the 2nd of July" said he.

"You are certainly an admirable witness" said Holmes "I may need some of these dates which you have noted"

"I learned method ~among other things~ from my great teacher. From the time that I ~began~ observed abnormality in his behaviour I felt that it was my duty to study his case. Thus I have it here that it was on that very day, July 2nd, that Roy attacked the Professor, as he came from his study into the Hall. Again on July 11th there was a scene of the same sort, and then I have a note of yet another upon ~June 23rd~ July 20th. After that we had to banish Roy to the Stables. He was a dear affectionate animal — but I fear I weary you"

Mr Bennett spoke in a tone of reproach for it was very clear that Holmes was not listening. His face was rigid and his eyes gazed abstractedly at the ceiling. With an effort he recovered himself.

"Singular! most singular!" he murmured. "These details were new to me. Mr Bennett. I think we have now fairly gone over the old ground, have we not? But you spoke of some fresh development"

The pleasant open face of our visitor clouded over, shadowed by some grim remembrance. "What I speak of occurred the night before last" said he **[Deletion of "I may explain that I was slept in town last night as I intended to see you today"[33]]** I was lying awake about two in the morning when I was aware of a dull muffled sound coming from the passage. I opened my door and peeped out. I should explain that the Professor sleeps at the end of the passage –

"The date being - ?" asked Holmes

Our visitor was clearly annoyed at so irrelevant **[Revised from 'irreverent'[34]]** an interruption.

"I have said, sir, that it was the night before last, that is Sept 4th."

Holmes nodded and smiled.

"Pray continue!" said he.

"He sleeps at the end of the passage and would have to pass my door in order to reach the staircase. It was

---

33 The revision removes a line that is both phrased rather clumsily, and also which muddles the chronology of the story. Without the amendment there would have been contradiction between the line which states that the events took place 'the night before last,' and the next line which sees Bennett sleeping 'in town last night.' Having said that, this is not the solution Doyle might have hoped. For by removing the second line and keeping to the idea of the dramatic events taking place 'the night before last' the reader is left with the curious silence of what happened during the day in between, and the unanswered question as to why Bennett did not come to see Holmes and Watson then.

34 This is a curious revision. Bearing in mind the succeeding lines depict Bennett as if he was annoyed with Holmes (for some unexplained reason), 'irreverent' fits much better than 'irrelevant.' Further, for Watson to say that Holmes asking for the date of events to be confirmed is 'irrelevant' makes little sense. It is almost as if Conan Doyle's initial idea for this section was to show Bennett as annoyed with the Great Detective, but then he decided against this - perhaps because within the narrative there really is no justification for such. At that point he then switched adjectives in order to tone down the annoyance of the young client, but then (for whatever reason) failed to remove the line where it is most clearly stated that Bennett is 'clearly annoyed.' Either way, the passage doesn't quite work - either Bennett is supposed to be annoyed, in which case some reason for this annoyance needs to be provided, or he is not supposed to be annoyed, and in which case the line that identifies him as such needs to be removed.

(52)

now fairly gone over the old ground, have we not? But you spoke of some fresh development"

The pleasant open face of our visitor clouded over, ~~ove~~ shadowed by some pain remembrance. "What I speak of occurred the night before last" said he "I may explain that I ~~was~~ slept in town last night as I intended ~~to see you~~ today. I was lying awake about two in the morning when I was aware of a dull muffled sound coming from the passage. I opened my door & peeped out. I should explain that the Professor sleeps at the end of the passage —

"The date being — ?" asked Holmes

Our visitor was clearly annoyed at so ~~unnecessary~~ irrelevant an interruption.

"I have said, sir, that it was the night before last, that is Sept 3rd 4th."

Holmes nodded and smiled.

"Pray continue!" said he.

"He sleeps at the end of the passage & would have to pass my door in order to reach the staircase. It was a really terrifying experience, Mr Holmes. I think I am as strong-nerved as my neighbours, but I was shaken by what I saw. The passage was dark save that one window half way along it threw a patch of light. I could see that something was coming along the passage, something dark and crouching. Then suddenly it emerged with the light and I saw that it was he. He was crawling, Mr Holmes – crawling! He was not quite on his hands and knees.[35] I should rather say on his hands and feet with his face sunk beneath his hands. Yet he seemed to move with ease. I was so paralysed by the sight that it was not until he reached my door that I was able to step forward and ask if I could assist him. His answer was extraordinary. He sprang up, spat out some atrocious word at me, and hurried on past me and down the staircase. I waited about for an hour but he did not come back. It must have been daylight before he regained his room"

"Well, Watson? What make you of that?" asked Holmes.

"Lumbago possibly.[36] I have known a severe attack make a man walk in just such a way, and nothing could be more trying to the temper"

---

35 The question of what the reader should infer at each point of the narrative, and how the intrigue and drama should be incrementally developed, is obviously central to 'The Creeping Man.' Many of the handwritten revisions are related to Doyle's attempts to build the suspense gradually. Thus it is noticeable here how he is doing his best to suggest the oddity of the Professor's behaviour, walking 'on his hands and knees,' without giving too much away.

36 Critics who quibble with 'The Creeping Man' on the basis of the supposed lesser quality of Conan Doyle's writing should all be pointed in the direction of Watson's suggested diagnosis here. It is an example of the sort of understated, beautifully observed dialogue that can only be written by a writer who is in tune with their characters. In those two words Doyle sums up all of Watson's rational professionalism, all of his matter-of-fact Englishness, and all of his tendency to remain forever slightly behind the curve.

a really terrifying experience, Mr Holmes. I think that I am as strong-nerved as my neighbours, but I was shaken by what I saw. The passage was dark save that one window half way along it threw a patch of light. I could see that something was coming along the passage, something dark & crouching. Then suddenly it emerged into the light and I saw that it was he. He was crawling, Mr Holmes — crawling! He was not quite on his hands and knees. I should rather say on his hands and feet with his face sunk beneath his hands. Yet he seemed to move with ease. I was so paralysed by the sight that it was not until he had reached my door that I was able to step forward and ask if I could assist him. His answer was extraordinary. He sprang up, spat out some atrocious word at me, and hurried on past ~~the~~ me and down the staircase. I waited about for an hour but he did not come back. It must have been daylight before he regained his room"

"Well, Watson? What make you of that?" asked Holmes.

"Lumbago possibly. I have known a severe attack make a man walk in just such a way," and nothing could be more trying to the temper"

"Good, Watson! You always keep us flatfooted on the ground. But we can hardly accept lumbago since he was able to stand erect in a moment"

"He was never better in health" said Bennett "In fact he is stronger than I have known him for years. But there are the facts, Mr Holmes. It is not a case in which we can consult the police, and yet we are utterly at our wits ends as to what to do, and we feel in some strange way that we are drifting towards disaster. Edith – Miss Presbury – feels as I do that we cannot wait passively any longer"

"It is certainly a very curious and suggestive case. What do you think, Watson?"

"Speaking as a medical man" said I "it appears to be a case for an alienist.[37] The old gentleman's cerebral processes were disturbed by the love affair. He made a journey abroad in the hope of breaking himself of the passion. His letters and the box may be connected with some other private transaction – a loan perhaps on[38] share certificates, **'which are in the box'**"[39]

"And the wolf-hound no doubt disapproved of the financial bargain **[Revised from 'terms' and possibly 'transaction'[40]]**. No, no, Watson, there is more in it than this.

---

37 An old-fashioned term, largely out-of-favour within modern medical professions. In broad terms it refers to professionals responsible for diagnosing conditions of the mind and/or personality. In particular, it has often been used to describe those who do so as part of criminal or forensic investigations.

38 In most published versions of the story this word is 'or' rather than 'on.' However, close inspection of the manuscript does suggest the latter rather than the former as Doyle's original choice.

39 It is apparent from the handwritten manuscript that this latter phrase was added later, in a different pen (or at least with the same pen when its ink level had changed significantly).

40 The revision appears to be a straightforward case of writerly preference for 'bargain' over 'terms' or 'transaction'; in terms of the meaning of the sentence, there is no significant change of emphasis.

"Good, Watson! You always keep us flat footed on the ground. But we can hardly accept lumbago since he was able to stand erect in a moment"

"He was never better in health" said Bennett "In fact he is stronger than I have known him for years. But there are the facts, Mr. Holmes. It is not a case in which we can consult the police, and yet we are utterly at our wits ends as to what to do, and we feel in some strange way that we are drifting towards disaster. Edith — Miss Presbury — feels as I do that we cannot wait passively any longer"

"It is certainly a very curious & suggestive case. What do you think, Watson?"

"Speaking as a medical man" said I "it appears to be a case for an alienist. The old gentleman's cerebral processes were disturbed by the love affair. He made a journey abroad in the hope of breaking himself of the passion. His letters and the box may be connected with some other private transaction — a loan perhaps on share certificates, "which are in the box"

"And the dog wolf-hound no doubt disapproved of the financial bargain. No, no, Watson, there is more in it than this.

Now I can only suggest –"

What Sherlock Holmes was about to suggest will never be known for at this moment the door was opened and a young lady shown into the room. As she appeared Mr Bennett sprang up with a cry and ran forward with his hands out to meet those which she had herself outstretched.

"Edith, dear! Nothing the matter, I hope?"

"I felt I must follow you. Oh, Jack,[41] I have been so dreadfully frightened! It is awful to be there alone"

"Mr Holmes, this is the young lady I spoke of. She is my fiancée"

"We were gradually coming to that conclusion, were we not, Watson?" Holmes answered with a smile. "I take it, Miss Presbury, that there was some fresh development in the case, and that you thought we should know"

Our new visitor, a bright handsome girl, of a conventional English type,[42] smiled back at Holmes as she seated herself beside Mr Bennett.

"When I found Mr Bennett had left his

---

41 Bennett's first name is of course Trevor. There have been numerous scholarly interpretations of this anomaly, but the most likely explanation is what D. Martin Dakin ('Second Thoughts on the Case-Book') calls the 'notorious carelessness' evident in some of Conan Doyle's narratives.

42 The description of Miss Presbury accords with the predominant stereotype of female identity during the Victorian period. Influenced by Coventry Patmore's 1854 poem of the same name, 'The Angel in the House' was an ideal of submissive femininity particularly associated with English middle-class identity, and embodying values of purity, duty, and chastity.

now I can only suggest ——"

What Sherlock Holmes was about to suggest will never be known for at this moment the door was opened and a young lady shown into the room. As she appeared Mr Bennett sprang up with a cry and ran forward with his hands out to meet those which she had herself outstretched.

"Edith, dear! Nothing the matter, I hope?"

"I felt I must follow you. Oh, Jack, I have been so dreadfully frightened! It is awful to be there alone"

"Mr. Holmes, this is the young lady I spoke of. This is my fiancée"

"We were gradually coming to that conclusion, were we not, Watson?" Holmes answered with a smile. "I take it, Miss Presbury, that there was some fresh development in the case, and that you thought we should know"

Our new visitor, a bright handsome girl, of a conventional English type, smiled back at Holmes as she seated herself beside Mr Bennett.

"When I found Mr Bennett had left his

hotel I thought I should probably find him here. Of course he had told me that he would consult you. But oh, Mr Holmes, can you do nothing for my poor father?"

"I have hopes, Miss Presbury, but the case is still obscure. Perhaps what you have to say may throw some fresh light upon it."

"It was last night, Mr Holmes. He had been very strange all day. I am sure that there are times when he has no recollection of what he does. He lives as in a strange dream. Yesterday was such a day. It was not father with whom I lived. His outward shell was there but it was not really he."

"Tell me what happened"

"I was awakened in the night by the dog barking most furiously.[43] Poor Roy, he is chained now near the stable. I may say that I always sleep with my door locked for as Jack – as Mr Bennett – will tell you we all have a feeling of impending danger. My room is on the second floor. It happened that the blind was up in my

---

43 In Sherlock Holmes stories the behaviour of animals as well as human relationships with animals are both often seen as clues within the wider deductive process. The most famous example of this is found in 'The Adventure of Silver Blaze' and its 'curious incident of the dog in the night-time.'

hotel I thought I should probably find him here. Ofcourse he had told me that he would consult you. But oh, Mr Holmes, can you do nothing for my poor father?"

"I have hopes, Miss Presbury, but the case is still obscure. Perhaps what you have to say may throw some fresh light upon it."

"It was last night, Mr Holmes. He had been very strange all day. I am sure that there are times when he has no recollection of what he does. He lives as in a strange dream. Yesterday was such a day. It was not my father with whom I lived. His outward shell was there but it was not really he."

"Tell me what happened"

"I was awakened in the night by the dog barking ˄ Poor ~~Carlo~~ Roy, he is chained now near the stable. I may say that I always sleep with my door locked for as Jack - as Mr Bennett - will tell you we all have a feeling of impending danger. My room is on the second floor. It happened that the blind was up in my

_{most furiously.}

window, and there was bright moonlight outside. As I lay with my eyes fixed upon the square of light, listening to the frenzied barkings[44] of the dog, I was amazed to see my father's face looking in at me. Mr Holmes, I nearly died of surprise and horror.[45] There it was pressed against the window pane and one hand seemed to be raised as if to push up the window. If that window had opened I think I should have gone mad. It was no delusion, Mr Holmes. Don't deceive yourself by thinking so. I daresay it was twenty seconds or so that I lay paralysed and watched the face. Then it vanished, but I could not – I could not, spring out of bed and look out after it. I lay cold and shivering till morning. At breakfast he was sharp and fierce in manner and made no allusion to the adventure of the night. Neither did I, but I gave an excuse for coming to town – and here I am.

Holmes looked thoroughly surprised at Miss Presbury's narrative.

"My dear young lady, you say that your room

---

44 Conan Doyle used the plural form in the original manuscript.
45 This incident is redolent with the sort of symbolic terror - a deranged man threatening to violate the intimate personal space of a chaste and pure young woman – which readers more usually find in the classical Gothic tradition of writers such as Matthew Lewis, Horace Walpole, or Ann Radcliffe.

window, and there was bright moonlight outside. As I lay with my eyes fixed upon the square of light, listening to the frenzied barkings of the dog, I was amazed to see my father's face looking in at me. Mr Holmes, I nearly died of surprise and horror. Then it was pressed against the window pane and one hand seemed to be raised as if to push up the window. If that window had opened I think I should have gone mad. It was no delusion, Mr. Holmes. Don't deceive yourself by thinking so. I daresay it was twenty seconds or so that I lay paralysed and watched the face. Then it vanished, but I could not — I could not, spring out of bed and look out after it. I lay cold and shivering till morning. At breakfast he was the sharp and fierce in manner ~~same as usual~~ and made no allusion to the adventure of the night. Neither did I, but I ~~made~~ gave an ~~any~~ excuse for coming to town — and here I am.

Holmes looked thoroughly surprised at Miss Presbury's narrative.

"My dear young lady, you say that your room

is on the second floor. Is there a long ladder in the garden?"

"No, Mr Holmes, that is the amazing part of it. There is no **[Deletion of 'possible'⁴⁶]** way of reaching the window – and yet he was there."⁴⁷

"The date being September 4th." said Holmes "That certainly complicates matters"

It was the young lady's turn to look surprised. "This is the second time that you have alluded to the date, Mr Holmes." said Bennett "Is it possible that it has any bearing upon the case?"

"It is possible – very possible – and yet I have not my full material **[Revised from 'data'⁴⁸]** at present."

"Possibly you are thinking of the connection between insanity and phases of the moon?"

"No, I assure you. It was quite a different line of thought. Possibly you can leave your notebook with me and I will check the dates. Now I think, Watson, that our line of action is perfectly clear. This young lady has informed us – and I have the greatest confidence in her intuition – that her

---

46 The revision gives the sentence greater accuracy – Presbury has indeed reached the window, so to claim that it is not 'possible' would be evidently false.
47 Readers who come to 'The Creeping Man' with knowledge of Edgar Allan Poe's 'The Murders in the Rue Morgue,' the story many critics identify as the first detective fiction, are likely to notice echoes of the way Poe depicts a similar window that no-one can supposedly access. And, likewise, in both stories the creature who is able to confound physics has ape/monkey-like tendencies.
48 The original term used sounds more scientific, and perhaps more in keeping with the Holmesian method. The precise reasons for the revision are unclear.

is on the second floor. Is there a long ladder in the garden?"

"No, Mr Holmes, that is the amazing part of it. There is no ~~possible~~ way of reaching the window — and yet he was there."

"The date being September 4th." said Holmes "That certainly complicates matters"

It was the young lady's turn to look surprised. "This is the second time that you have alluded to the date, Mr Holmes." said Bennett " Is it possible that it has any bearing upon the case?"

" It is possible — very possible — and yet I have not ~~my full~~ material ~~data~~ at present."

"Possibly you are thinking of the connection between insanity and phases of the moon?"

"No, I assure you. It was quite a different line of thought. Possibly you can leave your note book with me and I will check the dates. Now I think, Watson, that our line of action is perfectly clear. This young lady has informed us — and I have the greatest confidence in her intuition — that her father remembers little or nothing which occurs upon certain dates. We will therefore call upon him as if he had given us an appointment upon such a date. He will put it down to his own lack of memory. Thus we will open our campaign by having a good close view of him."

"That is excellent" said Mr Bennett. "I warn you however that the Professor is irascible and violent at times."

"[Deletion of 'And the sooner the better said'[49]] Holmes smiled.

"There are reasons why we should come at once – very cogent reasons if my theories hold good. Tomorrow, Mr Bennett, will certainly see us in Camford. There is, if I remember right, an inn called the Chequers where the port used to be above mediocrity, and the linen was above reproach.[50] I think, Watson, that our lot for the next few days might lie in less pleasant places."

Monday morning found us on our way to the famous university town – an easy effort on the part of Holmes who had no roots to pull up, but one which involved frantic planning and hurrying on my part, as my practise was by

---

49 This original phrase does not actually follow from what has been said by Bennett, which is probably why it has been deleted.
50 Holmes's knowledge of the level of service offered by up-market hostelries is indicative of his comfortable class position.

father remembers little or nothing which occurs upon certain dates. We will therefore call upon him as if he had given us an appointment upon such a date. He will put it down to his own lack of memory. Thus we will open our campaign by having a good close view of him."

"That is excellent" said Mr. Bennett. "I warn you however that the Professor is irascible and violent at times"

"And the sooner then better" said Holmes smiled. "There are reasons why we should come at once — very cogent reasons if my theories hold good. Tomorrow, Mr. Bennett, will certainly see us in Camford. There is, if I remember right, an inn called the Chequers where the port used to be above mediocrity, and the linen was above reproach. I think, Watson, that our lot for the next few days might lie in less pleasant places."

Monday morning found us on our way to the famous university town — an easy effort on the part of Holmes who had no roots to pull up, but one which involved frantic planning and hurrying upon my part, as my practice was by this time not inconsiderable. Holmes made no allusion to the case until after we had deposited our suit-cases at the ancient Hostel of which he had spoken.

"I think, Watson, that we can catch the Professor just before lunch. He lectures at eleven, and should have an interval at home."

"What possible excuse have we for calling?"

Holmes glanced at his notebook.

"There was a period of excitement upon August 26th. We will assume that he is a little hazy as to what he does at such times. If we insist that we are there by appointment I think he will hardly venture to contradict us.[51] Have you the effrontery necessary to put it through?"

"We can but try"

"Excellent Watson! Compound of the Busy Bee and Excelsior.[52] We can but try – the motto of the firm. A friendly native will surely guide us"

Such a one on the back of a smart Hansom swept us past a row of ancient colleges, and finally

---

51 As it turns out, Presbury does indeed contradict Holmes. Curiously, when he does so Holmes quickly seems to become confused, and forgets the original plan – which was to take advantage of the Professor's lapses in memory by pretending that a meeting had been previously arranged. Instead he unconvincingly claims that an anonymous third party *told* him that the Professor wished him to pay a visit, and an ugly confrontation between the two men ensues. It is difficult to comprehend how Conan Doyle allowed the narrative to wander off-track in this way, and why he did not tidy up the anomaly in subsequent versions of the story.

52 There is no definitive scholarly explanation as to the meaning of this phrase. The most detailed can be found in Klinger (ed.), 2005, p. 1649.

this time not inconsiderable. Holmes made no allusion to the case until after we had deposited our suit-cases at the ancient Hostel of which he had spoken.

"I think, Watson, that we can catch the Professor just before lunch. He lectures at eleven, and should have an interval at home."

"What possible excuse have we for calling?"

Holmes glanced at his note-book.

26th "There was a period of excitement upon August 26th. We will assume that he is a little hazy as to what he does at such times. If we insist that we are there by appointment I think he will hardly venture to contradict us. Have you the effrontery necessary to put it through?"

"We can but try"

"Excellent Watson! Compound of the busy bee & excelsior. We can but try – the motto of the firm. A friendly native will surely guide us"

Such a one on the back of a smart Hansom swept us past a row of ancient colleges, and finally turning into a tree-lined drive pulled up at the door of a charming house, girt round with lawns and covered with purple Wisteria.[53] Professor Presbury was certainly surrounded with every sign not only of comfort but of luxury. Even as we pulled up a grizzled head appeared at the front window, and we were aware of a pair of keen eyes from under shaggy brows which surveyed us through large horn glasses. A moment later we were actually in his sanctum, and the mysterious scientist whose vagaries had brought us from London, was standing before us. There was certainly no sign of eccentricity either in his manner or appearance, for he was a portly large-featured man, grave, tall and frockcoated, with the dignity of bearing which a lecturer needs. His eyes were his most remarkable feature, keen, observant and clever to the verge of cunning.

He looked at our cards. "Pray sit down, gentlemen. What can I do for you?"

Mr Holmes smiled amiably.

"It was the question which I was about to

---

53 The Wisteria flower is associated with a variety of symbolic meanings. However, if Conan Doyle is attempting to evoke any of these here then it is far from clear.

turning into a tree-lined drive pulled up at the door of a charming house, girt round with lawns and covered with purple Wisteria. Professor Presbury was certainly surrounded with every sign not only of comfort but of luxury. Even as we pulled up a grizzled head appeared at the front window, and we were aware of a pair of keen eyes from under shaggy brows which surveyed us through large horn glasses. A moment later we were actually in his Sanctum, and the mysterious Scientist whose vagaries had brought us from London, was standing before us. There was certainly no sign of eccentricity either in his manner or appearance, for he was a ~~kindly rosy-cheeked~~ portly large-featured man, grave, tall & frock coated, with the dignity of bearing which a lecturer needs. His eyes were his most remarkable feature, keen, observant and clever to the verge of cunning.

He looked at our cards. " Pray sit down, gentlemen. What can I do for you? "

Mr. Holmes smiled amiably.

" It was the question which I was about to

put to you, Professor?"

"To me, sir!"

"Possibly there is some mistake. I heard through a second person that Professor Presbury of Camford had need of my services"

"Oh indeed!" it seemed to me that there was a malicious sparkle in the intense gray[54] eyes. "You heard that, did you? May I ask the name of your informant?"

"I am sorry, Professor, but the matter was rather confidential. If I have made a mistake there is no harm done. I can only express my regret"[55]

"Not at all. I should wish to go further into this matter. It interests me. Have you any scrap of writing, any letter or telegram to bear out your assertion?"

"No, I have not."

"I presume that you do not go so far as to assert that I summoned you?"

"I would rather answer no questions" said Holmes.

"No, I dare say not" said the Professor with asperity. "However that particular one can be answered

---

54 This is Conan Doyle's original spelling.
55 This marks the point in the conversation where Holmes loses his focus (see footnote 51). He had intended to claim that a meeting had been arranged between the two of them, whereas instead he simply says 'I would rather answer no questions.'

put to you, Professor?"

"To me, sir!"

"Possibly there is some mistake. I heard through a second person that Professor Presbury of Camford had need of my services"

"Oh indeed!" It seemed to me that there was a malicious sparkle in the intense grey eyes. "You heard that, did you? May I ask the name of your informant?"

"I am sorry, Professor, but the matter was rather confidential. If I have made a mistake there is no harm done. I can only express my regret"

"Not at all. I should wish to go further into this matter. It interests me. Have you any scrap of writing, any letter or telegram to bear out your assertion?"

"No, I have not." ~~I presume that you do not go~~

"I presume that you do not go so far as to assert that I summoned you?"

"I would rather answer no questions" said Holmes.

"No. I dare say not" said the Professor with asperity. "However that particular one can be answered very easily without your aid"

He walked across the room to the bell. **[Deletion of 'As he did so Holmes turned swiftly to me'[56]]**

[Deletion of 'His knuckles' said he[57]]

[Deletion of 'The Professor's senses seemed singularly acute. "What was that?" has asked suspiciously. Before my friend could answer'[58]]

Our London friend Mr Bennett **[Deletion of 'had'[59]]** answered the call.

"Come in, Mr Bennett. These two gentlemen have come from London under the impression that they have been summoned. You handle all my correspondence. Have you a **[Revised from 'any'[60]]** note of anything going to a person named Holmes?"

"No, sir" **[Deletion of 'said'[61]]** Bennett answered with a flush.

"That is conclusive" said the Professor, glaring angrily at my Companion "Now, Sir – he leaned forward with his two hands upon the table "it seems to me that your position is a very questionable one"

[Deletion of 'Standing as he did my eyes full upon his knuckles. They were certainly extraordinary, though[62]

---

56 The revision would have significantly ratchetted up the tension at this point.
57 This would have more explicitly drawn the reader's attention to the nature of the Professor's condition.
58 Again, the mention of the acute hearing, coupled with that of his strange knuckles, would likely give the reader a much clearer sense of the Professor's sinister physicality.
59 The switch of tense gives the scene a greater immediacy.
60 A revision with a view to concision, otherwise with no substantive consequence.
61 The original formulation is a little more ponderous than the revision.
62 As with footnotes 56 and 57 above, Conan Doyle's first attempt reveals the drama of the scene more explicitly, rather than letting it build more slowly.

very easily without your aid "

He walked across the room to the bell. ~~as he did so~~
~~Holmes turned swiftly to me.~~

" ~~His knuckles " said he.~~

~~The Professor's senses seemed singularly acute "~~ What
was ~~that?~~ " he asked ~~suspiciously.~~ ~~Before my friend could~~
Holmes
~~answer~~ Our London friend Mr. Bennett ~~had~~ answered the
call.

" Come in, Mr. Bennett. These two gentlemen
have come from London under the impression that they have
been summoned. You handle all my correspondence. Have
you a note of anything going to a person named Holmes? "
answered
" No, sir " ~~and~~ Bennett, with a flush.

" That is conclusive " said the Professor,
glaring angrily at my companion " Now, sir — " he
leaned forward with his two hands upon the table " it
seems to me that your position is a very questionable one "

~~Standing as he did my eyes fell full upon~~
~~his knuckles. They were certainly extraordinary, though~~

only a man with my friend's rapid methods of observation might have noticed them. They seemed thick, hairy and discoloured.'[63]]

Holmes shrugged his shoulders.

"I can only repeat that I am sorry that we have made a needless intrusion."

"Hardy enough, Mr Holmes!" the old man cried in a high screaming voice with extraordinary malignancy upon his face. He got between us and the door as he spoke and he shook his two hands at us with furious passion "You can hardly get out of it so easily as that." His face was convulsed and he grinned and gibbered at us in his senseless rage.[64] I am convinced that we should have had to fight our way out of the room if Mr Bennett had not intervened.

"My dear Professor" he cried "Consider your position! Consider the scandal at the University! Mr Holmes is a well known man. You cannot possibly treat him with such discourtesy"

Sulkily our host – if I may call him so –

---

63 As with the previous footnote, 'hairy and discoloured' is much more explicit as to the nature of events.

64 The fact that the last part of this sentence was not edited out gives us a strong indication of where Conan Doyle felt the line needed to be drawn between revealing too much and revealing too little – he removed the sections that specifically mentioned the Professor's hairy knuckles, and which were (he must have felt) particularly indicative of monkey-like behaviour, yet chose to leave in 'grinned and gibbered at us in his senseless rage'; this must have been in the belief that the latter was suggestive yet measured.

only a man with my friend's rapid methods of observation might have noticed them. " They seemed thick, horny & discoloured.

Holmes shrugged his shoulders.

"I can only repeat that I am sorry that we have made a needless intrusion".

"Hardly enough, Mr Holmes !" The old man in a high screaming voice cried, with extraordinary malignancy upon his face. He got between us and the door as he spoke and he shook his two hands at us with furious passion " You can hardly get out of it so easily as that." His face was convulsed and he grinned and gibbered at us in his senseless rage. I am convinced that we should have had to fight our way out of the room if Mr Bennett had not intervened.

" My dear Professor" he cried " Consider your position ! Consider the scandal at the University ! Mr Holmes is a well known man. You cannot possibly treat him with such discourtesy"

Sulkily our host – if I may call him so –

cleared the path to the door. We were glad to find ourselves outside the house and in the quiet of the tree lined drive. Holmes seemed gently amused by the episode.

"Our learned friend's nerves are somewhat out of order" said he "Perhaps our intrusion was a little crude and yet we have gained that personal contact which I desired. **[Deletion of 'You say his hands. Suggestive, were they not?'[65]]**

[Deletion of "Of what, Holmes?"

"Ah, that is where our little problem lies. The knuckles were abnormal – that at least is evident. But[66]]

But dear me, Watson, he is surely at our heels. The villain still pursues us"

There were the sounds of running feet behind but it was, to my relief, not the formidable professor but his assistant who appeared round the curve of the drive. He came panting up to us.

"I am so sorry, Mr Holmes. I wished to apologise"

---

65   The amendment accords with others whereby Conan Doyle removed specific mention of the Professor's hands.
66   As with footnote 65 and elsewhere.

cleared the path to the door. We were glad to find ourselves
outside the house and in the quiet of the tree lined drive.
Holmes seemed gently amused by the episode.

"Our learned friend's nerves are some what out
of order" said he "Perhaps our intrusion was a little
crude and yet we have gained that personal contact
which I desired. ~~You saw his hands. Suggestive, were
they not?~~"

"Of what, Holmes?"

"~~Ah, that is where our little problem lies. The
knuckles were abnormal — that at least is evident. But~~ But
dear me, Watson, he is surely at our heels. The villain
still pursues us"

There were the sounds of running feet
behind ~~us~~ but it was, to my relief, not the formidable
professor but his assistant who appeared round the curve
of the drive. He came panting up to us.

"I am so sorry, Mr. Holmes. I wished to
apologise"

"Mr dear sir, there is no need. It is all in the way of professional experience"

"I have never seen him in a more dangerous a mood. But he grows more sinister. You can understand now why his daughter and I are alarmed. And yet his mind is perfectly clear"

"Too clear!" said Holmes "That was my miscalculation. It is evident that his memory is much more reliable that I had thought.[67] By the way can we before we go see the window of Miss Presbury's room?"

Mr Bennett pushed his way through some shrubs and we had a view of the side of the house.

"It is there. The second on the left"

"Dear me, it seems hardly accessible. And yet you will observe that there is a creeper below and a water pipe above which give some foothold"[68]

"I could not climb it myself" said Mr Bennett.

"Very likely. It would certainly be a

---

67 This sentence assumes that Holmes followed his original plan and tried to fool Presbury into thinking that the two men had arranged a meeting, using the Professor's own lapses in memory against him. But because that never happens this comment is entirely out of place. It is as if Conan Doyle has overlooked entirely that the narrative developed rather differently from planned.

68 For Poe enthusiasts, another echo of 'The Murders at the Rue Morgue,' perhaps?

"My dear sir, there is no need. It is all in the way of professional experience"

"I have never seen him in a more dangerous a mood. But he grows more sinister. You can understand now why his daughter and I are alarmed. And yet his mind is perfectly clear"

"Too clear!" said Holmes "That was my miscalculation. It is evident that his memory is much more reliable than I had thought. By the way can we before we go see the window of Miss Presbury's room?"

Mr Bennett pushed his way through some shrubs and we had a view of the side of the house.

"It is there — The second on the left"

"Dear me, it seems hardly accessible. And yet you will observe that there is a creeper below & a water pipe above which give some foot hold"

"I could not climb it myself" said Mr Bennett.

"Very likely. It would certainly be a

dangerous exploit for any normal man."

"There was one other thing I wished to tell you, Mr Holmes. I have the address of the man in London to whom the Professor writes. He seems to have written this morning and I got it from his blotting paper. It is an ignoble position for a trusted secretary but what else can I do?"

Holmes glanced at the paper, and put it into his pocket.

"Dorak – a curious name. Slavonic, I imagine.[69] Well, it is an important link in the chain. We return to London this afternoon, Mr Bennett. I see no good purpose to be served by our remaining. We cannot arrest the Professor because he has done no crime, nor can we place him under constraint for he cannot be proved to be mad. No action is as yet possible."

"Then what on earth are we to do?"

"A little patience, Mr Bennett. Things

---

69 The choice of surname, as with the choice of Prague and the use of foreign-ness throughout the story, resonates with suspicion and Gothic intrigue.

dangerous exploit for any normal man."

"There was one other thing I wished to tell you, Mr Holmes. I have the address of the man in London to whom the Professor writes. He seems to have written this morning and I got it from his blotting paper. It is an ignoble position for a trusted secretary but what else can I do.[2]"

Holmes glanced at the paper, and put it into his pocket.

"Dorak - a curious name. Slavonic, I imagine. Well, it is an important link in the chain. We return to London this afternoon, Mr Bennett. I see no good purpose to be served by our remaining. We cannot arrest the Professor because he has done no crime, nor can we place him under constraint for he cannot be proved to be mad. No action is as yet possible."

"Then what on earth are we to do?"

"A little patience, Mr Bennett. Things

will soon develop. Unless I am mistaken next Saturday may mark a crisis. Certainly we shall be in Camford on that day. Meanwhile the general position is certainly unpleasant, and if Miss Presbury can prolong her visit -"

"That is easy"

"Then let her stay till we can assure her that all danger is past. Meanwhile let him have his way and do not cross him. So long as he is in a good humour all is well."

"There he is!" cried Bennett is a startled whisper. Looking between the branches we saw the tall erect figure emerge from the hall door and look around him. He stood leaning forwards, his hands swinging straight before him, his head turning from side to side. The secretary with a last wave slipped off among the trees, **[Deletion of 'which we rapidly made our way down to the gate and to lunch at our hotel. The same evening saw us back in Baker Street once more.'[70]]** and we saw him presently rejoin his employer, the two entering the house together in what seemed to be animated and even excited conversation.

---

70 The sentence that has been removed would have brought forward the return of Holmes and Watson to Baker Street. That the author chose to revise this is perhaps an indication that, on reflection, he realised it was more convenient for the development of the narrative if they remained in Camford.

will soon develope. Unless I am mistaken next
Saturday may mark a crisis. Certainly we shall be in
Camford on that day. Meanwhile the general position is
certainly unpleasant, and if Miss Presbury can
prolong her visit — "

       "That is easy"

       " Then let her stay till we can assure her
that all danger is past. Meanwhile let him have his
way and do not cross him. So long as he is in a
good humour all is well."

       "There he is!" cried Bennett in a startled
whisper. Looking between the branches we saw the
tall erect figure emerge from the hall door & look
around him. He stood leaning forwards, his
hands swinging straight before him, his head
turning from side to side. The secretary with a
last wave slipped off among the trees, ~~while we~~ and we saw
him presently rejoin his employer, the two entering the house
~~rapidly made our way down to the gate & so~~
together in what seemed to be animated and even excited conver-
~~back to our Hotel, the same evening and so back~~
-sation.
~~in Baker Street once asked.~~

"I expect the old gentleman has been putting two and two together" said Holmes, as we walked hotel wards.

"He struck me as having a particularly clear, logical brain, from the little I saw of him. Explosive, no doubt, but then from his point of view he has something to explode about if detectives are put on his track and he suspects his own household of doing it. I rather fancy that friend Bennett is in for an uncomfortable time"

Holmes stopped at a post office and sent off a telegram on our way. The answer reached us in the evening and he tossed it across to me. "Have visited the Commercial Road[71] and seen Dorak. Suave person, Bohemian, elderly. Keeps large general store. Mercer"

"Mercer is since your time" said Holmes "He is my general utility man who looks up routine business.[72] It was important to know something of the man with whom our Professor was so secretly corresponding. His nationality connects up with the Prague visit"

"Thank goodness that something connects

---

71 Commercial Road is located in the East End of London, running from Tower Hamlets in the East, through Limehouse and ending at its junction with Whitechapel High Street at its most westerly point. The East End of London has historically been home to poor working-class and immigrant communities, drawn to the area by employment opportunities in and around the docks.

72 The fact that Holmes sees 'Mercer' as a regular and ongoing feature of his investigations, and that Watson is unfamiliar with him, establishes clearly that their personal and professional lives have become almost entirely separate by this point.

"I expect the old gentleman has been putting two and two together" said Holmes, as we walked hotel wards. "He struck me as having a particularly clear, logical brain, from the little I saw of him. Explosive, no doubt, but then from his point of view he has something to explode about if detectives are put on his track and he suspects his own household of doing it. I rather fancy that friend Bennett is in for an uncomfortable time"

Holmes stopped at a post office and sent off a telegram on our way. The answer reached us in the evening and he tossed it across to me. "Have visited the Commercial Road and seen Dorak. Suave person, Bohemian, elderly. Keeps large general store. Mercer"

"Mercer is since your time" said Holmes "He is my general utility man who looks up routine business. It was important to know something of the man with whom our Professor was so secretly corresponding. His nationality connects up with the Prague visit"

"Thank goodness that something connects

with something" said I "at present we seem to be faced by a long series of inexplicable incidents with no bearing upon each other. For example what possible connection can there be between an angry wolf-hound **[Revised from 'elderly spaniel']**[73] and a visit to Bohemia,[74] or either of them with a man crawling down a passage at night! As to your dates that is the biggest mystification of all."

Holmes smiled and rubbed his hands. We were, I may say, seated in the old sitting room of the ancient hotel with a bottle of the famous vintage of which Holmes had spoken, on the table between us.

"Well now, let us take the dates first" said he, his fingertips together and his manner as if he were addressing a class. "This excellent young man's diary shows that there was trouble **[Revised from 'weekly']**[75] at nine day intervals, with so far as I remember only one exception. Thus the last outbreak upon Friday **[Revised from 'Saturday']**[76] was on Sept 3rd which also falls into the series, as did Aug 26th which preceded it. The thing is beyond coincidence"

---

73 As the narrative moves towards a dramatic denouement, in which the dog plays a prominent role, Conan Doyle's motivation for changing 'Roy' from a spaniel to a wolf-hound becomes clear.

74 A further instance where Doyle draws on a sense of Gothic foreign-ness as a clear counterpoint to the rational, scientific Englishness embodied by Holmes and Watson.

75 This revision is part of Conan Doyle's wider attempts to delineate a clear, consistent chronology of events within the story.

76 As with the previous footnote, dates and days are revised to keep to a consistent narrative chronology.

with something" said I. "At present we seem to be faced by a long series of inexplicable incidents with no bearing upon each other. For example what possible connection can there be between an angry ~~collie~~ wolf-hound spaniel and a visit to Bohemia, or either of them with a man crawling down a passage at night? As to your dates that is the biggest mystification of all."

Holmes smiled and rubbed his hands. We were, I may say, seated in the ~~dim~~ old sitting room of the ancient Hotel with a bottle of the famous vintage of which Holmes had spoken, on the table between us.

"Well now, let us take the dates first" said he, his finger tips together and his manner as if he were addressing a class. "This excellent young man's diary shows that there was trouble upon July 2, and from then onwards it seems to have been ~~weekly~~ at nine day intervals, with so far as I remember only one exception. Thus the last outbreak upon ~~Saturday~~ friday was on Sept 3d ~~22~~ which also falls into the ~~weekly~~ series, as did Aug 26 ~~29~~ which preceded it. The thing is beyond coincidence"

I was forced to agree.

"Let us then form the provisional theory that every 9 days **[Revised from 'once a week, upon Fridays'[77]]** the Professor takes some strong drug which has a passing but highly poisonous[78] effect. His naturally violent nature is intensified by it. He learned to take this drug while he was in Prague and is now supplied with it by a Bohemian intermediary in London. This all hangs together, Watson"

"But the dog, the face at the window, the creeping man in the passage?"

"Well, well, we have made a beginning. I should not expect any fresh developments until next Tuesday. In the mean time we can only keep in touch with friend Bennett, and enjoy the amenities of this charming University town."[79]

In the morning Mr Bennett slipped round to bring us the latest report. As Holmes had imagined times had not been easy with him. Without actually accusing him of being responsible for our presence the Professor had been very rough and rude in his speech, and evidently felt some strong grievance.

---

77   Another example of Conan Doyle's adjustments so as to maintain a consistent narrative chronology.

78   By the end of the story it is not entirely clear whether this assumption is correct – strictly speaking, there is no actual evidence that the serum the Professor injects is poisonous. It appears to change his behaviour, personality and physical capacities, and Holmes offers a doom-laden warning about how such interventions in the evolutionary process endanger the human species. However, the question as to whether the serum is actually poisonous remains unanswered.

79   This sentence is one of the oddities of the story. Coming as it does just after Holmes's tense summary of the case so far, such a hearty recommendation to 'enjoy the amenities of this charming town' jars awkwardly, and feels decidedly un-Holmesian in tone and sentiment.

I was forced to agree.

"Let us then form the provisional theory that once a week, upon ~~postage~~ the Professor takes some strong drug which has a passing but highly poisonous effect. His naturally violent nature is intensified by it. He learned to take this drug while he was in Prague and is now supplied with it by a Bohemian inter- -mediary in London. This all hangs together, Watson."

"But the dog, the face at the window, the creeping man in the passage?"

"Well, well, we have made a beginning. I should not expect any fresh developments until next ~~Friday~~ tuesday. In the mean time we can only keep in touch with friend Bennett, and enjoy the amenities of this charming University town."

In the morning Mr. Bennett slipped round to bring us the latest report. As Holmes had imagined times had not been easy with him. Without exactly accusing him of being responsible for our presence the Professor had been very rough - rude in his speech, and evidently felt some strong grievance.

(interlinear: every 9 days)

This morning he was quite himself again however and had delivered his usual brilliant lecture to a crowded class. "Apart from his queer fits" said Bennett "he has actually more energy and vitality than I can ever remember, nor was his brain ever clearer. But its not he - its never the man whom we have known"

"I don't think you have anything to fear now for a week at least" Holmes answered "I am a busy man and Dr Watson has his patients to attend to. Let us agree that we meet here at this hour next Tuesday and I shall be surprised if before we leave you again we are not able to explain even if we cannot perhaps put an end to your troubles. Meanwhile keep us posted in what occurs."[80]

I saw nothing of my friend for the next few days, but on the following Monday evening I had a short note asking me to meet him next day at the train. From what he told me as we travelled up to Camford all was well, the peace of the Professor's house had been unruffled, and his own conduct perfectly normal.

---

80 This paragraph feels a little half-hearted, as if its sole reason for being is to move the narrative on hurriedly towards the conclusion.

This morning he was quite himself again however and had delivered his usual brilliant lecture to a crowded class. "Apart from his queer fits" said Bennett "he has actually more energy and vitality than I can ever remember, nor was his brain ever clearer. But its not he — its never the man whom we have known"

"I don't think you have anything to fear now for a week at least" Holmes answered. "I am a busy man and Dr Watson has his patients to attend to. Let us agree that we meet here at this hour next tuesday and I shall be surprised if before we leave you again we are not able to explain even if we cannot perhaps put an end to your troubles. Meanwhile keep us posted in what occurs."

I saw nothing of my friend for the next few days, but on the following monday evening I had a short note asking me to meet him next day at the train. From what he told me as we travelled up to Camford all was well, the peace of the Professor's house had been unruffled, and his own conduct perfectly normal.

This also was the report which was given to us by Mr Bennett himself when he called upon us that evening at our old quarters in the Chequers.

"He heard from his London correspondent today. There was a letter and there was a small packet each with the cross under the stamp which warned me not to touch them. There has been nothing else"

"That may prove quite enough" said Holmes grimly "Now, Mr Bennett, we shall I think, come to some conclusion tonight. If my conclusions are correct we should have an opportunity of bringing matters to a head. In order to do so it is necessary to hold the Professor under observation. I would suggest therefore that you remain awake and on the lookout. Should you hear him pass your door do not interrupt him but follow him as discreetly as you can.[81] Dr Watson and I will not be far off. By the way where is the key of that little box of which you spoke?"

"Upon his watchchain"

"I fancy our researches must lie in that direction. At the worst the lock should not be very formidable. Have you any other able-bodied man on the premises?"

There is the Coachman Macphail"

---

81 Conan Doyle never explains why the Professor's medication causes him to be entirely oblivious to his surroundings in this way.

This also was the report which was given us by Mr. Bennett himself when he called upon us that evening at our old quarters in the Chequers. "He heard from his London correspondent today. There was a letter and there was a small packet each with the cross under the stamp which warned me not to touch them. There has been nothing else."

"That may prove quite enough" said Holmes grimly "Now, Mr. Bennett, we shall, I think, come to some conclusion tonight. If my conclusions are correct we should have an opportunity of bringing matters to a head. In order to do so it is necessary to hold the Professor under observation. I would suggest therefore that you remain awake and on the look out. Should you hear him pass your door do not interrupt him but follow him as discreetly as you can. Dr. Watson and I will not be far off. By the way where is the key of that little box of which you spoke?"

"Upon his watch chain"

"I fancy our researches must lie in that direction. At the worst the lock should not be very formidable. Have you any other able-bodied man on the premises?"

"There is the Coachman Macphail"

"Where does he sleep?"

"Over the Stables"

"We might possibly want him. Well we can do no more until we see how things develop. Goodbye – but I expect that we shall see you before morning."

It was nearly midnight before we took our station among some bushes immediately opposite the hall door of the Professor. It was a fine night, but chilly, and we were glad of our warm overcoats. There was a breeze and clouds were scudding across the sky, obscuring from time to time the half moon. It would have been a dismal vigil were it not for the expectation and excitement which carried us along, and the assurance of my comrade that we had probably reached the end of the strange sequence of events which had engaged our attention.

"If the cycle of nine days holds good then we shall have the Professor at his worst tonight" said Holmes "The fact that these strange symptoms began after his visit to Prague,[82] that he is in secret correspondence with a Bohemian dealer in London,[83]

---

82 As is often the case in the Sherlock Holmes canon, a visit to a foreign location is thus the precursor to notable, undesirable changes in personality.

83 The narrative implies that secrecy is necessary because this sort of immoral practice is proscribed in England, being incompatible with the upright moral values of the British Empire.

" Where does he sleep ? "

" Over the Stables "

" We might possibly want him. Well we can do no
more until we see how things develope. Goodbye — but I expect
that we shall see you before morning."

It was nearly midnight before we took our station
among some bushes immediately opposite the hall door of the
Professor. It was a fine night, but chilly, and we were glad of our
warm overcoats. There was a breeze and clouds were scudding
across the sky, obscuring from time to time the half moon. It
would have been a dismal vigil were it not for the expectation a
excitement which carried us along, and the assurance of my
comrade that we had probably reached the end of the strange
sequence of events which had engaged our attention.

" If the cycle of nine days holds good then we shall
have the Professor at his worst tonight " said Holmes " The fact
that these strange symptoms began after his visit to Prague, that
he is in secret correspondence with a Bohemian dealer in London,

who presumably represents someone in Prague, and that he received a packet from him this very day, all point in one direction. What he takes and why he takes it is still beyond our ken, but that it emanates in some way from Prague is clear enough. He takes it under definite directions which regulate this ninth day system which was the first point which attracted my attention. But his symptoms are most remarkable. Did you observe his knuckles?"[84]

I had to confess that I did not.

"Thick and hairy in a way which is quite new in my experience. Always look at the hands first, Watson. Then cuffs, trouserknees and boots. Very curious knuckles which can only be explained by the mode of progression observed by" – Holmes paused, and suddenly clapped his hand to his forehead "Oh, Watson, Watson, what a fool I have been! It seems incredible and yet it must be true. All points in one direction. How could I miss seeing this connection of ideas! Those knuckles – how could I have passed those knuckles! And the dog! And the ivy!

---

84 At this point in the narrative, in Conan Doyle's original manuscript, the specific references to Professor Presbury's monkey-like knuckles are not removed, whereas they had been earlier. Doyle becomes more explicit in his descriptions, with a view to building up to the dramatic conclusion. As such these revisions bear witness to Doyle's skill as a storyteller through his decisions on what to reveal, and when, in order to incrementally ratchet up the drama and tension.

who presumably represents some one in Prague, and that he received a packet from him this very day, all point in one direction. What he takes and why he takes it is still beyond our ken, but that it emanates in some way from Prague is clear enough. He takes it under definite directions which regulate this ninth day system which was the first point which attracted my attention. But his symptoms are most remarkable. Did you observe his knuckles?"

I had to confess that I did not.

"Thick and horny in a way which is quite new in my experience. Always look at the hands first, Watson. Then cuffs, trouser knees and boots. Very curious knuckles which can only be explained by the mode of progression observed by —" Holmes paused, and suddenly clapped his hand to his forehead " Oh, Watson, Watson, what a fool I have been! It seems incredible and yet it must be true. All points in one direction. How could I miss seeing the connection of ideas! Those knuckles — how could I have passed those knuckles! And the dog! And the ivy!

It's surely time that I disappeared with that little farm of my dreams.[85] Look out, Watson! Here he is! We will have the chance of seeing for ourselves."

The hall door had slowly opened, and against the lamp-lit background we saw the tall figure of Professor Presbury. He was clad in his dressing ground.[86] As he stood outlined in the doorway he was erect but leaning forward with dangling arms, as when we saw him last. Now he stepped forward into the drive and an extraordinary change came over him. He sank down into a crouching position and moved along upon his hands and feet, skipping every now and then as if he were overflowing with energy and vitality[87]. He moved along the face of the house and then round the corner. As he disappeared Bennett slipped through the hall door and softly followed him.

"Come, Watson, come!" cried Holmes, and we slipped as softly as we could through the bushes until we had gained a spot whence we could see the other side of the house, which was bathed in the light of the half moon. The Professor

---

85 Another example of the sort of eloquence which critics rarely associate with the stories of *The Case-Book.*
86 Clearly the wrong word is used by accident here – it should be 'dressing-gown.'
87 Unlike other mentions of the supposedly positive physiological effects of Presbury's medication, Conan Doyle chose not to delete this one.

It's surely time that I disappeared into that little farm of my dreams. Look out, Watson! Here he is! We will have the chance of seeing for ourselves."

The hall door had slowly opened, and against the lamp-lit background we saw the tall figure of Professor Presbury. He was clad in his ~~ordinary~~ dressing grown. As he stood outlined in the doorway he was erect but leaning forward with dangling arms, as when we saw him last. Now he stepped forward into the drive and an extraordinary change came over him. He sank down into a crouching position & moved along upon his hands and feet, skipping every now & then as if he were overflowing with energy and vitality. He moved along the face of the house and then round the corner. As he disappeared Bennett ~~off~~ slipped through the hall door and softly followed him.

"Come, Watson, come!" cried Holmes, and we slipped as softly as we could through the bushes until we had gained a spot whence we could see the other side of the house, which was bathed in the light of the half moon. The Professor was clearly visible crouching at the foot of the ivy-covered wall. As we watched him he suddenly began with incredible agility to ascend it. From branch to branch he sprang, sure of foot and firm of grasp, climbing apparently in mere joy at his own prowess with no definite object in view. With his dressing gown flapping on each side of him he looked like some huge bat[88] glued against the side of his own house, a great square dark patch upon the moonlit wall. Presumably he tired of this amusement and dropping from branch to branch he squatted down with the old attitude and moved towards the stables, creeping along in the same strange way as before. The wolf hound was out now, barking furiously, and more excited than ever when it actually caught sight of its master. It was straining on its chain and quivering with eagerness and rage. The Professor squatted down very deliberately just out of reach of the hound, and began to provoke it in every possible way.[89] He took handfuls of pebbles from the drive and threw them in the dog's face, prodded him with a stick which he had picked up, flicked his hands about only a few inches from the gaping mouth, and endeavouring in every

---

88 Once again Conan Doyle draws on classic Gothic iconography as he heightens the drama of the narrative.

89 It is unclear whether Doyle's representation of 'monkey-like' behaviour is based on any particular first-hand knowledge he might have had, from observing monkeys in the wild or within zoos. It is possible that his sense of how monkeys behave is more speculative, in the same way as his representation of exotic wildlife elsewhere in the Sherlockian canon, such as his wonderfully bizarre portrayal of cheetahs, baboons and snakes in 'The Speckled Band.'

was clearly visible crouching at the foot of the wall ivy-covered wall. As we watched him he suddenly began with incredible agility to ascend it. From branch to branch he sprang, sure of foot & firm of grasp, climbing apparently in mere joy at his own powers with no definite object in view. With his dressing gown flapping on each side of him he looked like some huge bat glued against the side of his own house, a great square dark patch upon the moonlit wall. Presently he tired of this amusement and dropping ~~down~~ from branch to branch he squatted down into the old attitude and moved towards the stables, creeping along in the same strange way as before. The wolf hound was out now, barking furiously, and more excited than ever when it actually caught sight of its master. It was straining on its chain and quivering with eagerness and rage. The Professor squatted down very deliberately just out of reach of the hound, and began to provoke it in every possible way. He took handfuls of pebbles from the drive and threw them in the dog's face, goaded him with a stick which he had picked up, flicked his hands about only a few inches from the gaping mouth, and endeavouring in every way to increase the animal's fury which was already beyond all control. In all our adventures I do not know that I have ever seen a more strange sight than this impassive and still dignified figure crouching froglike upon the ground and goading the maddened hound which ramped and raged in front of him by all manner of ingenious and calculated cruelty to a wilder exhibition of passion.

And then in a moment it happened! It was not the chain that broke but it was the collar that slipped for it had been made for a thick-necked Newfoundland.[90] We heard the rattle of falling metal and the next instant dog and man were rolling on the ground together, the one roaring in rage, the other screaming in a strange shrill falsetto of terror. It was a very narrow thing for the Professor's life. The savage creature had him fairly by the throat, its fangs had bitten deep,[91] and he was senseless before we could reach them and drag the two apart. It might have been a dangerous task for us, but Bennetts voice and presence brought the giant wolf hound instantly to reason. The uproar had brought the sleepy and

---

90 This information poses a number of questions that the narrative never answers. First, whose dog was the Newfoundland? Second, why is it that Roy does not have his own chain/collar? And third, if the collar was too big for a Wolfhound - to the point that when provoked he is able to slip out of it - then how is it that he did not force an escape previously? Especially as the narrative makes clear that the nocturnal habits of Professor Presbury have greatly disturbed Roy on numerous other occasions, and anyone who knows anything about dog breeds will know that the differences in body and neck size between a Wolfhound and a Newfoundland are significant enough for such an escape to have been relatively easy at any point.

91 It is arguable that Conan Doyle might have done better to choose a more fearsome breed of dog than a Wolfhound to play the role of this 'savage creature;' that said, in comparison to the original version of 'Roy,' who was a faithful spaniel, the Wolfhound does at least offer *some* Gothic potential. Avid readers of Holmes will notice how the end of 'The Creeping Man' has obvious echoes of the conclusion of 'The Copper Beeches,' wherein Carlo the mastiff viciously attacks his master Jephro Rucastle.

way to encrease the animal's fury which was already beyond all control. In all our adventures I do not know that I have ever seen a more strange sight than this impassive & still dignified figure crouching froglike upon the ground and goading the maddened hound which rampd and raged in front of him by all manner of ingenious & calculated cruelty to a wilder exhibition of passion.

And then in a moment it happened! It was not the chain that broke but it was the collar that slipped for it had been made for a thick-necked Newfoundland. We heard the rattle of falling metal and the next instant dog and man were rolling on the ground together, the one roaring in rage, the other screaming in a strange shrill falsetto of terror. It was a very narrow thing for the Professor's life. The savage creature had him fairly by the throat, its fangs had bitten deep, and he was senseless before we could reach them & drag the two apart. It might have been a dangerous task for us, but Bennetts voice and presence brought the great wolf hound instantly to reason. The uproar had brought the sleepy and astonished Coachman from his room above the stables. "I'm not surprised" said he, shaking his head "I've seen him at it before. I knew the dog would get him sooner or later."

The hound was secured and together we carried the Professor up to his room where Bennett, who had a medical degree, helped me to dress his torn throat. The sharp teeth had passed dangerously near the carotid artery and the haemorrhage was serious. In half an hour the danger was passed.[92] I had given the patient an injection of morphine and he had sunk into deep sleep. Then, and only then were we able to look at each other and to take stock of the situation.

"I think a first class surgeon should see him" said I.[93]

"For God's sake no!" cried Bennett "At present the scandal is confined to our own household. It is safe with us. If it gets beyond these walls it will never stop. Consider his position at the University, his European reputation,

---

92 The drama in this part of the narrative is significantly underplayed. It feels rushed, as if Conan Doyle is trying to force things quickly to a conclusion. The dramatic potential of the Professor's 'torn throat' is resolved within half-an-hour, and in no more than one brief sentence.

93 Sherlockian scholars have drawn attention to what appears to be Watson's loss of faith in his own medical abilities here; Robert Katz calls it a 'startling admission' ('John H. Watson, M.D.: The Non-Surgical Surgeon'). There has, however, been less focus on the precise meaning of Watson's words - in particular, bearing in mind it has already been conceded that the 'danger was passed,' what particular procedure(s) does Watson have in mind for a 'first-class surgeon' to perform?

astonished Coachman from his room above the stables. "I'm
not surprised" said he, shaking his head "I've seen him
too at it before. I knew the dog would get him sooner or
later."

The hound was secured and together we
carried the Professor up to his room where Bennett, who had
a medical degree, helped me to dress his torn throat. The
sharp teeth had passed dangerously near the carotid artery
and the hemorrhage was serious. In half an hour the
danger was passed. I had given the patient an injection
of morphia and he had sunk into deep sleep. Then, and
only then were we able to look at each other and to take
stock of the situation.

"I think a first class surgeon should see him"
said I.

"For God's sake no!" cried Bennett "At
present the scandal is confined to our own household. It is safe
with us. If it gets beyond these walls it will never stop.
Consider his position at the University, his European reputation,

the feelings of his daughter"

"Quite so" said Holmes "I think it may be quite possible to keep the matter to ourselves, and also to prevent its recurrence now that we have a free hand. The key from the watch chain, Mr Bennett. John will guard the patient and let us know if there is any change. Let us see what we can find in the Professor's mysterious box"

There was not much but there was enough – an empty phial, another nearly full, a hypodermic syringe, several letters in a crabbed foreign hand. The marks on the envelopes showed that they were those which had disturbed the routine of the secretary, and each was dated from the Commercial Road and signed A Dorak. They were mere invoices to say that a fresh bottle was being sent to Professor Presbury, or receipts to acknowledge money. There was one other envelope however in a more educated hand and bearing the Austrian **[Revised from 'Bohemian'[94]]** stamp with the post-mark of Prague. "Here we have our material!" cried Holmes, as he tore out the enclosure.

---

94 This change perhaps indicates a sudden realization, on Conan Doyle's part, that at the time the story is set Bohemia was actually part of the wider Austro-Hungarian empire. Or, perhaps it was simply an attempt to imply a wider European involvement in the questionable scientific practices which feature in the story.

the feelings of his daughter"

"Quite so" said Holmes "I think it may be quite possible to keep the matter to ourselves, and also to prevent its recurrence now that we have a free hand. The key from the watch chain, Mr. Bennett. John will guard the patient and let us know if there is any change. Let us see what we can find in the Professor's mysterious box"

There was not much but there was enough— an empty phial, another nearly full, a hypodermic syringe, several letters in a crabbed foreign hand. The marks on the envelopes showed that they were those which had disturbed the routine of the secretary, and each was dated from the Commercial Road and signed A Dorak. They were mere invoices to say that a fresh bottle was being sent to Professor Presbury, or receipts to acknowledge money. There was one other envelope however in a more educated hand and bearing the ~~Bohemian~~ Austrian stamp with the post-mark of Prague. "Here we have our material!" cried Holmes, as he tore out the enclosure.

"Honoured Colleague" it ran "Since your esteemed visit I have thought much of your case, and though in your circumstances there are some special reasons for the treatment, I would none the less enjoin caution, as my results have shown that it is not without danger of a kind.

It is possible that the serum of Anthropoid[95] would have been better. I have, as I explained to you, used Black-faced Langur[96] because a specimen was available. Langur is of course a crawler and climber while Anthropoid walks erect, and is in all ways nearer.

I beg you to take every possible precaution that there be no premature revelation of the process. I have one other Client in England, and Dorak is my agent for both.

Weekly reports will oblige

Yours with high esteem.

H. Lowenstein.[97]

Lowenstein! The name brought back to me the memory of some snippet from a newspaper which spoke of an obscure scientist who was striving in some inhuman way for the secret

---

95 In general this term is used to refer to higher forms of primate, especially with a human-like form. However, Lowenstein appears to be referring specifically to forms of anthropoid that would in his view have been more effective subjects in his scientific experimentation, such as (the reader might reasonably assume) Gorillas or Chimpanzees.

96 The 'black-faced' or 'gray' Langur are relatively small, long-tailed monkeys, mainly native to wooded areas of the Indian sub-continent. They walk/run on all fours, are prolific jumpers and climbers, and are both diurnal and herbivorous.

97 A number of Sherlockian scholars have attempted to 'prove' the real-life identity of 'Lowenstein.' Prager and Silverstein ('Lowenstein of Prague: The Most Maligned Man in the Canon'), for example, identify him as Austrian scientist Eugen Steinach; whereas Rodin and Key (*Medical Casebook of Dr Arthur Conan Doyle*) relate the science of 'The Creeping Man' to the work of the Frenchman Charles-Édouard Brown-Séquard. As I make clear in the 'Introduction' to this volume, in reality there were numerous experimental scientists engaged in parallel projects related to the type of science featured in this story. As such, the likelihood is that Lowenstein is an aggregate of many/all of these, and that he is a symbol of a type of science and type of scientist, rather than being a model of any one person in particular.

"Honoured Colleague" it ran "Dear Since your esteemed visit I have thought much of your case, and though in your circumstances there are some special reasons for the treatment, I would none the less enjoin caution, as my results have shown that it is not without danger of a kind.

It is possible that the serum of Anthropoid would have been better. I have, as I explained to you, used Black-faced Langur because a specimen was accessible. Langur is of-course a crawler and climber while Anthropoid walks erect, and is in all ways nearer.

I beg you to take every possible precaution that there be no premature revelation of the process. I have one other client in England, and Dorak is my agent for both.

Weekly reports will oblige

Yours with high esteem.

H. Lowenstein.

Lowenstein! The name brought back to me the memory of some snippet from a newspaper which spoke of an obscure scientist who was striving in some unknown way for the secret of rejuvenescence and the elixir of life.[98] Lowenstein of Prague! Lowenstein with the wondrous strength-giving serum, tabooed by the profession because he refused to reveal its source. In a few words I said what I remembered. Bennett had taken a manual of zoology from the shelves. "'Langur" he read "the great black-faced monkey of the Himalayan slopes, biggest and most human of climbing monkeys.' Many details are added. Well thanks to you. Mr Holmes, it is very clear that we have traced the evil to its source".

"The real source" said Holmes "lies of course in that untimely love affair which gave an impetuous Professor the idea that he could only gain his wish by turning himself into a younger man.[99] When one tries to rise above nature one is liable to fall below it. The highest type of man can revert to the animal if he leaves the straight road of destiny."[100] He sat musing for a little with the phial in his hand, looking at the clear liquid within. "When I have written to this man and told him

---

98   See the 'Introduction' to this volume for a consideration of so-called 'elixir of life' myths.

99   Belief in such rejuvenative science was, at the time Conan Doyle was writing 'The Creeping Man,' widespread. This is discussed in the 'Introduction' to this volume.

100 Here Holmes is conflating a broader sense of destiny with the sort of biological determinism that, by the earlier twentieth century, had become a largely unchallenged feature of evolutionary thinking. His view is that Professor Presbury mistakenly interferes in the 'inevitable' evolutionary process. Such interference with 'normal' evolutionary processes is thus associated with a reversion or retrogression of the individual and species. Which, for a man who prides himself on his scientific process, is logically absurd. If it were true then thousands of years of development in medical treatments for all number of ailments, conditions and impairments, all of which take humankind away from the pure path of the 'survival of the fittest,' are damned by implication as unwarranted interruptions to the evolutionary process that will reverse the progress of the species.

of rejuvenescence and the elixir of life. Lowenstein of
Prague! Lowenstein with the wondrous strength-giving
serum, tabooed by the Profession because he refused to reveal
its source. In a few words I said what I remembered.
Bennett had taken a manual of zoology from the shelves.
"Langur" he read "the great black-faced monkey of the
Himalayan slopes, biggest and most human of climbing
monkeys". Many details are added. Well thanks to you, Mr.
Holmes, it is very clear that we have traced the evil to its
source".

            "The real source" said Holmes " lies of course
in that untimely love affair which gave our impetuous
Professor the idea that he could only gain his wish by
turning himself into a younger man. When one tries to
rise above Nature one is liable to fall below it. The highest
type of man can revert to the animal if he leaves the
straight road of destiny." He sat musing for a little
with the phial in his hand, looking at the clear liquid
within. " When I have written to this man & told him

that I hold him criminally responsible for the poisons which he circulates, we will have no more trouble. But it may recur. Others may find a better way. There is danger there – a very real danger to humanity. Consider, Watson, that the material, the sensual, the worldly would all prolong their worthless lives.[101] The spiritual would not avoid the call to something higher.[102] It would be the survival of the least fit.[103] What sort of cess-pool may not our poor world become." Suddenly the dreamer disappeared, and Holmes the man of action sprang from his chair. "I think there is nothing more to be said, Mr Bennett. The various incidents will now fit themselves easily into the general scheme. The dog of course was aware of the change far more quickly than you. His smell would insure that. It was the monkey not the Professor whom Roy attacked, just as it was the monkey who teased Roy. Climbing was a joy to the creature and it was a mere chance, I take it, that the pastime brought him to the young ladies' window.

---

101 These words are unusually harsh, even for Holmes. They indicate a bleak view of humankind – perhaps not surprising in a story written in the aftermath of the Great War. However, they also seem to indicate the stirrings of a belief in Eugenics – founded in the idea that some lives are more valuable than others, that some examples of the species are more valuable than others, and thus that the 'chosen' ones should be given priority when it comes to procreation.

102 This is a very ambiguous sentence. Doyle implies an opposition, even tension, between the 'material' and the 'spiritual' worlds, which readers might not find surprising from a man who by this point in his career was one of the leading lights of the international Spiritualist movement. What is not clear, however, is how Holmes is relating the supposedly 'spiritual' people to his wider concern with the morality of human interference in the evolutionary process.

103 This paraphrase of the 'survival of the fittest' is the most explicit allusion to evolutionary thought within the story. Holmes implies that those who use science in such dubious ways, who interfere in the pre-destined evolutionary processes through a selfish desire to live longer, more vital lives, are the 'least fit' of the species. If unchecked they will, Holmes claims, create a 'cess-pool' of their kind.

that I hold him criminally responsible for the poisons which he circulates, we will have no more trouble. But it may recur. Others may find a better way. There is danger there — a very real danger to humanity. Consider, Watson, that the material, the sensual, the worldly would all prolong their worthless lives. The spiritual would not avoid the call to something higher. It would be the survival of the least fit. What sort of cess-pool may not our poor world become." Suddenly the dreamer disappeared, and Holmes the man of action sprang from his chair " I think there is nothing more to be said, Mr. Bennett. The various incidents will now fit themselves easily into the general scheme. The dog of course was aware of the change far more quickly than you. His smell would ensure that. It was the monkey not the Professor whom Roy attacked, just as it was the monkey who teased Roy. Climbing was a joy to the creature and it was a mere chance, I take it, that the pastime brought him to the young ladies' window.

There is an early train to town, Watson, but I think we shall just have time for a cup of tea at the Chequers before we catch it"

Arthur Conan Doyle

Crowborough[104]

---

104 Conan Doyle and his second wife Jean Leckie moved into Windlesham, their expensively-renovated Sussex home - Doyle came to call it 'Swindlesham' – towards the end of 1907, soon after they were married.

" There is an early train to Town, Watson, but I think we shall just have time for ~~one~~ a cup of tea at the Chequers before we catch it "

Arthur Conan Doyle
    Crowborough

THE ADVENTURE OF THE CREEPING MAN

A NEW SHERLOCK HOLMES STORY

BY

A. Conan Doyle

ILLUSTRATED BY
HOWARD ELCOCK

MR. SHERLOCK HOLMES was always of opinion that I should publish the singular facts connected with Professor Presbury, if only to dispel once for all the ugly rumours which some twenty years ago agitated the University and were echoed in the learned societies of London. There were, however, certain obstacles in the way, and the true history of this curious case remained entombed in the tin box which contains so many records of my friend's adventures. Now we have at last obtained permission to ventilate the facts which formed one of the very last cases handled by Holmes before his retirement from practice. Even now a certain reticence and discretion have to be observed in laying the matter before the public.

It was one Sunday evening early in September of the year 1902 that I received one of Holmes's laconic messages : "Come at once if convenient—if inconvenient come all the same.—S. H." The relations between us in these latter days were peculiar. He was a man of habits, narrow and concentrated habits, and I had become one of them. As an institution I was like the violin, the shag tobacco, the old black pipe, the index books, and others perhaps less

excusable. When it was a case of active work and a comrade was needed upon whose nerve he could place some reliance, my *rôle* was obvious. But apart from this I had uses. I was a whetstone for his mind. I stimulated him. He liked to think aloud in my presence. His remarks could hardly be said to be made to me—many of them would have been as appropriately addressed to his bedstead—but none the less, having formed the habit, it had become in some way helpful that I should register and interject. If I irritated him by a certain methodical slowness in my mentality, that irritation served only to make his own flame-like intuitions and impressions flash up the more vividly and swiftly. Such was my humble *rôle* in our alliance.

When I arrived at Baker Street I found him huddled up in his arm-chair with up-drawn knees, his pipe in his mouth and his brow furrowed with thought. It was clear that he was in the throes of some vexatious problem. With a wave of his hand he indicated my old arm-chair, but otherwise for half an hour he gave no sign that he was aware of my presence. Then with a start he seemed to come from his reverie, and, with his usual whimsical smile, he greeted me back to what had once been my home.

" You will excuse a certain abstraction of mind, my dear Watson," said he. " Some curious facts have been submitted to me within the last twenty-four hours, and they in turn have given rise to some speculations of a more general character. I have serious thoughts of writing a small monograph upon the uses of dogs in the work of the detective."

" But surely, Holmes, this has been explored," said I. " Bloodhounds—sleuth-hounds——"

" No, no, Watson ; that side of the matter is, of course, obvious. But there is another which is far more subtle. You may recollect that in the case which you, in your sensational way, coupled with the Copper Beeches, I was able, by watching the mind of the child, to form a deduction as to the criminal habits of the very smug and respectable father."

" Yes, I remember it well."

" My line of thoughts about dogs is analogous. A dog reflects the family life. Whoever saw a frisky dog in a gloomy family, or a sad dog in a happy one ? Snarling people have snarling dogs, dangerous people have dangerous ones. And their passing moods may reflect the passing moods of others."

I shook my head. " Surely, Holmes, this is a little far-fetched," said I.

He had refilled his pipe and resumed his seat, taking no notice of my comment.

" The practical application of what I have said is very close to the problem which I am investigating. It is a tangled skein, you understand, and I am looking for a loose end. One possible loose end lies in the question : Why does Professor Presbury's faithful wolf-hound, Roy, endeavour to bite him ? "

I sank back in my chair in some disappointment. Was it for so trivial a question as this that I had been summoned from my work ? Holmes glanced across at me.

" The same old Watson ! " said he. " You never learn that the gravest issues may depend upon the smallest things. But is it not on the face of it strange that a staid, elderly philosopher—you've heard of Presbury, of course, the famous Camford physiologist ?—that such a man, whose friend has been his devoted wolf-hound, should now have been twice attacked by his own dog ? What do you make of it ? "

" The dog is ill."

" Well, that has to be considered. But he attacks no one else, nor does he apparently molest his master, save on very special occasions. Curious, Watson—very curious. But young Mr. Bennett is before his time, if that is his ring. I had hoped to have a longer chat with you before he came."

THERE was a quick step on the stairs, a sharp tap at the door, and a moment later the new client presented himself. He was a tall, handsome youth about thirty, well dressed and elegant, but with something in his bearing which suggested the shyness of the student rather than the self-possession of the man of the world. He shook hands with Holmes, and then looked with some surprise at me.

" This matter is very delicate, Mr. Holmes," he said. " Consider the relation in which I stand to Professor Presbury, both privately and publicly. I really can hardly justify myself if I speak before any third person."

" Have no fear, Mr. Bennett. Dr. Watson is the very soul of discretion, and I can assure you that this is a matter in which I am very likely to need an assistant."

" As you like, Mr. Holmes. You will, I am sure, understand my having some reserves in the matter."

" You will appreciate it, Watson, when I tell you that this gentleman, Mr. Trevor Bennett, is professional assistant to the great scientist, lives under his roof, and is engaged to his only daughter. Certainly we must agree that the Professor has every claim upon his loyalty and devotion. But it may best be shown by taking the necessary steps to clear up this strange mystery."

" I hope so, Mr. Holmes. That is my one object. Does Dr. Watson know the situation ? "

" I have not had time to explain it."

" Then perhaps I had better go over the ground again before explaining some fresh developments."

" I will do so myself," said Holmes, " in order to show that I have the events in their due order. The Professor, Watson, is a man of European reputation. His life has been academic. There has never been a breath of scandal. He is a widower with one daughter, Edith. He is, I gather, a man of very virile and positive, one might almost say combative, character. So the matter stood until a very few months ago.

" Then the current of his life was broken. He is sixty-one years of age, but he became engaged to the daughter of Professor Morphy, his colleague in the chair of Comparative Anatomy. It was not, as I understand, the reasoned courting of an elderly man, but rather the passionate frenzy of youth, for no one could have shown himself a more devoted lover. The lady, Alice Morphy, was a very perfect girl both in mind and body, so that there was every excuse for the Professor's infatuation. None the less, it did not meet with full approval in his own family."

" We thought it rather excessive," said our visitor.

"Exactly. Excessive and a little violent and unnatural. Professor Presbury was rich, however, and there was no objection upon the part of the father. The daughter, however, had other views, and there were already several candidates for her hand, who, if they were less eligible from a worldly point of view, were at least more of an age. The girl seemed to like the Professor in spite of his eccentricities. It was only age which stood in the way.

"About this time a little mystery suddenly clouded the normal routine of the Professor's life. He did what he had never done before. He left home and gave no indication where he was going. He was away a fortnight, and returned looking rather travel-worn. He made no allusion to where he had been, although he was usually the frankest of men. It chanced, however, that our client here, Mr. Bennett,

received a letter from a fellow-student in Prague, who said that he was glad to have seen Professor Presbury there, although he had not been able to talk to him. Only in this way did his own household learn where he had been.

"Now comes the point. From that time onwards a curious change came over the Professor. He became furtive and sly.

There was a sharp tap at the door, and a moment later the new client presented himself.

Those around him had always the feeling that he was not the man that they had known, but that he was under some shadow which had darkened his higher qualities. His intellect was not affected. His lectures were as brilliant as ever. But always there was something new, something sinister and unexpected. His daughter, who was devoted to him, tried again and again to resume the old relations and to penetrate this mask which her father seemed to have put on. You, sir, as I understand, did the same—but all was in vain. And now, Mr. Bennett, tell in your own words the incident of the letters."

"You must understand, Dr. Watson, that the Professor had no secrets from me. If I were his son or his younger brother, I could not have more completely enjoyed his confidence. As his secretary I handled every paper which came to him, and I opened and subdivided his letters. Shortly after his return all this was changed. He told me that certain letters might come to him from London which would be marked by a cross under the stamp. These were to be set aside for his own eyes only. I may say that several of these did pass through my hands, that they had the E.C. mark, and were in an illiterate handwriting. If he answered them at all the answers did not pass through my hands nor into the letter-basket in which our correspondence was collected."

"And the box," said Holmes.

"Ah, yes, the box. The Professor brought back a little wooden box from his travels. It was the one thing which suggested a Continental tour, for it was one of those quaint carved things which one associates with Germany. This he placed in his instrument cupboard. One day, in looking for a canula, I took up the box. To my surprise he was very angry, and reproved me in words which were quite savage for my curiosity. It was the first time such a thing had happened and I was deeply hurt. I endeavoured to explain that it was a mere accident that I had touched the box, but all the evening I was conscious that he looked at me harshly and that the incident was rankling in his mind." Mr. Bennett drew a little diary book from his pocket. "That was on the 2nd of July," said he.

"You are certainly an admirable witness," said Holmes. "I may need some of these dates which you have noted."

"I learned method among other things from my great teacher. From the time that I observed abnormality in his behaviour I felt that it was my duty to study his case. Thus I have it here that it was on that very day, July 2nd, that Roy attacked the Professor as he came from his study into the hall. Again on July 11th there was

a scene of the same sort, and then I have a note of yet another upon July 20th. After that we had to banish Roy to the stables. He was a dear, affectionate animal—but I fear I weary you."

MR. BENNETT spoke in a tone of reproach, for it was very clear that Holmes was not listening. His face was rigid and his eyes gazed abstractedly at the ceiling. With an effort he recovered himself.

"Singular ! Most singular ! " he murmured. " These details were new to me, Mr. Bennett. I think we have now fairly gone over the old ground, have we not ? But you spoke of some fresh development."

The pleasant, open face of our visitor clouded over, shadowed by some grim remembrance. " What I speak of occurred the night before last," said he. " I was lying awake about two in the morning, when I was aware of a dull muffled sound coming from the passage. I opened my door and peeped out. I should explain that the Professor sleeps at the end of the passage——"

" The date being—— ? " asked Holmes.

Our visitor was clearly annoyed at so irrelevant an interruption.

" I have said, sir, that it was the night before last—that is, September 4th."

Holmes nodded and smiled.

" Pray continue," said he.

" He sleeps at the end of the passage, and would have to pass my door in order to reach the staircase. It was a really terrifying experience, Mr. Holmes. I think that I am as strong-nerved as my neighbours, but I was shaken by what I saw. The passage was dark save that one window half-way along it threw a patch of light. I could see that something was coming along the passage, something dark and crouching. Then suddenly it emerged into the light, and I saw that it was he. He was crawling, Mr. Holmes—crawling ! He was not quite on his hands and knees. I should rather say on his hands and feet, with his face sunk between his hands. Yet he seemed to move with ease. I was so paralysed by the sight that it was not until he had reached my door that I was able to step forward and ask if I could assist him. His answer was extraordinary. He sprang up, spat out some atrocious word at me, and hurried on past me and down the staircase. I waited about for an hour, but he did not come back. It must have been daylight before he regained his room."

" Well, Watson, what make you of that ? " asked Holmes, with the air of the pathologist who presents a rare specimen.

" Lumbago, possibly. I have known a

severe attack make a man walk in just such a way, and nothing would be more trying to the temper."

"Good, Watson! You always keep us flat-footed on the ground. But we can hardly accept lumbago, since he was able to stand erect in a moment."

"He was never better in health," said Bennett. "In fact, he is stronger than I have known him for years. But there are the facts, Mr. Holmes. It is not a case in which we can consult the police, and yet we are utterly at our wits' end as to what to do, and we feel in some strange way that we are drifting towards disaster. Edith—Miss Presbury—feels as I do, that we cannot wait passively any longer."

"It is certainly a very curious and suggestive case. What do you think, Watson?"

"Speaking as a medical man," said I, "it appears to be a case for an alienist. The old gentleman's cerebral processes were disturbed by the love affair. He made a journey abroad in the hope of breaking himself of the passion. His letters and the box may be connected with some other private transaction—a loan, perhaps, or share certificates, which are in the box."

"And the wolf-hound no doubt disapproved of the financial bargain. No, no, Watson, there is more in it than this. Now, I can only suggest——"

WHAT Sherlock Holmes was about to suggest will never be known, for at this moment the door opened and a young lady was shown into the room. As she appeared Mr. Bennett sprang up with a cry and ran forward with his hands out to meet those which she had herself outstretched.

"Edith, dear! Nothing the matter, I hope?"

"I felt I must follow you. Oh, Jack, I have been so dreadfully frightened! It is awful to be there alone."

"Mr. Holmes, this is the young lady I spoke of. This is my *fiancée*."

"We were gradually coming to that conclusion, were we not, Watson?" Holmes answered, with a smile. "I take it, Miss Presbury, that there is some fresh development in the case, and that you thought we should know?"

Our new visitor, a bright, handsome girl of a conventional English type, smiled back at Holmes as she seated herself beside Mr. Bennett.

"When I found Mr. Bennett had left his hotel I thought I should probably find him here. Of course, he had told me that he would consult you. But, oh, Mr. Holmes, can you do nothing for my poor father?"

"I have hopes, Miss Presbury, but the case is still obscure. Perhaps what you have to say may throw some fresh light upon it."

"It was last night, Mr. Holmes. He had been very strange all day. I am sure that there are times when he has no recollection of what he does. He lives as in a strange dream. Yesterday was such a day. It was not my father with whom I lived. His outward shell was there, but it was not really he."

"Tell me what happened."

"I was awakened in the night by the dog barking most furiously. Poor Roy, he is chained now near the stable. I may say that I always sleep with my door locked; for, as Jack—as Mr. Bennett—will tell you, we all have a feeling of impending danger. My room is on the second floor. It happened that the blind was up in my window, and there was bright moonlight outside. As I lay with my eyes fixed upon the square of light, listening to the frenzied barkings of the dog, I was amazed to see my father's face looking in at me. Mr. Holmes, I nearly died of surprise and horror. There it was pressed against the window-pane, and one hand seemed to be raised as if to push up the window. If that window had opened, I think I should have gone mad. It was no delusion, Mr. Holmes. Don't deceive yourself by thinking so. I dare say it was twenty seconds or so that I lay paralysed and watched the face. Then it vanished, but I could not—I could not spring out of bed and look out after it. I lay cold and shivering till morning. At breakfast he was sharp and fierce in manner, and made no allusion to the adventure of the night. Neither did I, but I gave an excuse for coming to town—and here I am."

Holmes looked thoroughly surprised at Miss Presbury's narrative.

"My dear young lady, you say that your room is on the second floor. Is there a long ladder in the garden?"

"No, Mr. Holmes; that is the amazing part of it. There is no possible way of reaching the window—and yet he was there."

"The date being September 4th," said Holmes. "That certainly complicates matters."

It was the young lady's turn to look surprised. "This is the second time that you have alluded to the date, Mr. Holmes," said Bennett. "Is it possible that it has any bearing upon the case?"

"It is possible—very possible—and yet I have not my full material at present."

"Possibly you are thinking of the connection between insanity and phases of the moon?"

"No, I assure you. It was quite a different line of thought. Possibly you can

The Professor spat out some atrocious word at me and hurried on down
the staircase.

leave your note-book with me and I will check the dates. Now I think, Watson, that our line of action is perfectly clear. This young lady has informed us—and I have the greatest confidence in her intuition—that her father remembers little or nothing which occurs upon certain dates. We will therefore call upon him as if he had given us an appointment upon such a date. He will put it down to his own lack of memory. Thus we will open our campaign by having a good close view of him."

"That is excellent," said Mr. Bennett. "I warn you, however, that the Professor is irascible and violent at times."

Holmes smiled. "There are reasons why we should come at once—very cogent reasons if my theories hold good. To-morrow, Mr. Bennett, will certainly see us in Camford. There is, if I remember right, an inn called the Chequers where the port used to be above mediocrity, and the linen was above reproach. I think, Watson, that our lot for the next few days might lie in less pleasant places."

Monday morning found us on our way to the famous University town—an easy effort on the part of Holmes, who had no roots to pull up, but one which involved frantic planning and hurrying on my part, as my practice was by this time not inconsiderable. Holmes made no allusion to the case until after we had deposited our suit-cases at the ancient hostel of which he had spoken.

"I think, Watson, that we can catch the Professor just before lunch. He lectures at eleven, and should have an interval at home."

"What possible excuse have we for calling?"

Holmes glanced at his note-book.

"There was a period of excitement upon August 26th. We will assume that he is a little hazy as to what he does at such times. If we insist that we are there by appointment I think he will hardly venture to contradict us. Have you the effrontery necessary to put it through?"

"We can but try."

"Excellent, Watson! Compound of the Busy Bee and Excelsior. We can but try—the motto of the firm. A friendly native will surely guide us."

Such a one on the back of a smart hansom swept us past a row of ancient colleges, and finally turning into a tree-lined drive pulled up at the door of a charming house, girt round with lawns and covered with purple wistaria. Professor Presbury was certainly surrounded with every sign not only of comfort but of luxury. Even as we pulled up a grizzled head appeared at the front window, and we were aware of a pair of keen eyes from under shaggy brows which surveyed us through large horn glasses. A moment later we were actually in his sanctum, and the mysterious scientist, whose vagaries had brought us from London, was standing before us. There was certainly no sign of eccentricity either in his manner or appearance, for he was a portly, large-featured man, grave, tall, and frock-coated, with the dignity of bearing which a lecturer needs. His eyes were his most remarkable feature, keen, observant, and clever to the verge of cunning.

He looked at our cards. "Pray sit down, gentlemen. What can I do for you?"

Mr. Holmes smiled amiably.

"It was the question which I was about to put to you, Professor."

"To me, sir!"

"Possibly there is some mistake. I heard through a second person that Professor Presbury of Camford had need of my services."

"Oh, indeed!" It seemed to me that there was a malicious sparkle in the intense grey eyes. "You heard that, did you? May I ask the name of your informant?"

"I am sorry, Professor, but the matter was rather confidential. If I have made a mistake there is no harm done. I can only express my regret."

"Not at all. I should wish to go further into this matter. It interests me. Have you any scrap of writing, any letter or telegram, to bear out your assertion?"

"No, I have not."

"I presume that you do not go so far as to assert that I summoned you?"

"I would rather answer no questions," said Holmes.

"No, I dare say not," said the Professor, with asperity. "However, that particular one can be answered very easily without your aid."

HE walked across the room to the bell. Our London friend, Mr. Bennett, answered the call.

"Come in, Mr. Bennett. These two gentlemen have come from London under the impression that they have been summoned. You handle all my correspondence. Have you a note of anything going to a person named Holmes?"

"No, sir," Bennett answered, with a flush.

"That is conclusive," said the Professor, glaring angrily at my companion. "Now, sir"—he leaned forward with his two hands upon the table—"it seems to me that your position is a very questionable one."

Holmes shrugged his shoulders.

"I can only repeat that I am sorry that we have made a needless intrusion."

"Hardly enough, Mr. Holmes!" the old man cried, in a high screaming voice, with extraordinary malignancy upon his face. He got between us and the door as he spoke, and he shook his two hands at us with furious passion. "You can hardly get out of it so easily as that." His face was convulsed and he grinned and gibbered at us in his senseless rage. I am convinced that we should have had to fight our way out of the room if Mr. Bennett had not intervened.

"My dear Professor," he cried, "consider your position! Consider the scandal at the University! Mr. Holmes is a well-known man. You cannot possibly treat him with such discourtesy."

Sulkily our host—if I may call him so—cleared the path to the door. We were glad to find ourselves outside the house, and in the quiet of the tree-lined drive. Holmes seemed amused by the episode.

"Our learned friend's nerves are somewhat out of order," said he. "Perhaps our intrusion was a little crude, and yet we have gained that personal contact which I desired. But, dear me, Watson, he is surely at our heels. The villain still pursues us."

There were the sounds of running feet behind, but it was, to my relief, not the formidable Professor but his assistant who appeared round the curve of the drive. He came panting up to us.

"I am so sorry, Mr. Holmes. I wished to apologize."

"My dear sir, there is no need. It is all in the way of professional experience."

"I have never seen him in a more dangerous mood. But he grows more sinister. You can understand now why his daughter and I are alarmed. And yet his mind is perfectly clear."

"Too clear!" said Holmes. "That was my miscalculation. It is evident that his memory is much more reliable than I had thought. By the way, can we, before we go, see the window of Miss Presbury's room?"

Mr. Bennett pushed his way through some shrubs and we had a view of the side of the house.

"It is there. The second on the left."

"Dear me, it seems hardly accessible. And yet you will observe that there is a creeper below and a water pipe above which give some foothold."

"I could not climb it myself," said Mr. Bennett.

"Very likely. It would certainly be a dangerous exploit for any normal man."

"There was one other thing I wished to tell you, Mr. Holmes. I have the address of the man in London to whom the Professor writes. He seems to have written this morning and I got it from his blotting paper. It is an ignoble position for a trusted secretary, but what else can I do?"

Holmes glanced at the paper and put it into his pocket.

"Dorak—a curious name. Slavonic, I imagine. Well, it is an important link in the chain. We return to London this afternoon, Mr. Bennett. I see no good purpose to be served by our remaining. We cannot arrest the Professor because he has done no crime, nor can we place him under constraint, for he cannot be proved to be mad. No action is as yet possible."

" Then what on earth are we to do ? "

" A little patience, Mr. Bennett. Things will soon develop. Unless I am mistaken next Tuesday may mark a crisis. Certainly we shall be in Camford on that day. Meanwhile, the general position is undeniably unpleasant, and if Miss Presbury can prolong her visit——"

" That is easy."

" Then let her stay till we can assure her that all danger is past. Meanwhile let him have his way and do not cross him. So long as he is in a good humour all is well."

" There he is ! " said Bennett, in a startled whisper. Looking between the branches we saw the tall, erect figure emerge from the hall door and look around him. He stood leaning forward, his hands swinging straight before him, his head turning from side to side. The secretary with a last wave slipped off among the trees, and we saw him presently rejoin his employer, the two entering the house together in what seemed to be animated and even excited conversation.

" I expect the old gentleman has been putting two and two together," said Holmes, as we walked hotel-wards. " He struck me as having a particularly clear and logical brain, from the little I saw of him. Explosive, no doubt, but then from his point of view he has something to explode about if detectives are put on his track and he suspects his own household of doing it. I rather fancy that friend Bennett is in for an uncomfortable time."

Holmes stopped at a post-office and sent off a telegram on our way. The answer reached us in the evening, and he tossed it across to me. " Have visited the Commercial Road and seen Dorak. Suave person, Bohemian, elderly. Keeps large general store.—Mercer."

" Mercer is since your time," said Holmes. " He is my general utility man who looks up routine business. It was important to know something of the man with whom our Professor was so secretly corresponding. His nationality connects up with the Prague visit."

" Thank goodness that something connects with something," said I. " At present we seem to be faced by a long series of inexplicable incidents with no bearing upon each other. For example, what possible connection can there be between an angry wolf-hound and a visit to Bohemia, or either of them with a man crawling down a passage at night ? As to your dates, that is the biggest mystification of all."

Holmes smiled and rubbed his hands. We were, I may say, seated in the old sitting-room of the ancient hotel, with a bottle of the famous vintage of which Holmes had spoken on the table between us.

" Well, now, let us take the dates first," said he, his finger-tips together and his manner as if he were addressing a class. " This excellent young man's diary shows that there was trouble upon July 2nd, and from then onwards it seems to have been at nine-day intervals, with, so far as I remember, only one exception. Thus the last outbreak upon Friday was on September 3rd, which also falls into the series, as did August 26th, which preceded it. The thing is beyond coincidence."

I was forced to agree.

" Let us, then, form the provisional theory that every nine days the Professor takes some strong drug which has a passing but highly poisonous effect. His naturally violent nature is intensified by it. He learned to take this drug while he was in Prague, and is now supplied with it by a Bohemian intermediary in London. This all hangs together, Watson ! "

" But the dog, the face at the window, the creeping man in the passage ? "

" Well, well, we have made a beginning. I should not expect any fresh developments until next Tuesday. In the meantime we can only keep in touch with friend Bennett and enjoy the amenities of this charming town."

IN the morning Mr. Bennett slipped round to bring us the latest report. As Holmes had imagined, times had not been easy with him. Without exactly accusing him of being responsible for our presence, the Professor had been very rough and rude in his speech, and evidently felt some strong grievance. This morning he was quite himself again, however, and had delivered his usual brilliant lecture to a crowded class. " Apart from his queer fits," said Bennett, " he has actually more energy and vitality than I can ever remember, nor was his brain ever clearer. But it's not he—it's never the man whom we have known."

" I don't think you have anything to fear now for a week at least," Holmes answered. " I am a busy man, and Dr. Watson has his patients to attend to. Let us agree that we meet here at this hour next Tuesday, and I shall be surprised if before we leave you again we are not able to explain, even if we cannot perhaps put an end to, your troubles. Meanwhile, keep us posted in what occurs."

I SAW nothing of my friend for the next few days, but on the following Monday evening I had a short note asking me to meet him next day at the train. From

220

The Professor's face was convulsed and he
rage. I am convinced that Holmes and I
room if Mr. Bennett

what he told me as we travelled up to
Camford all was well, the peace of the
Professor's house had been unruffled, and
his own conduct perfectly normal. This
also was the report which was given us by
Mr. Bennett himself when he called upon
us that evening at our old quarters in the
Chequers. "He heard from his London
correspondent to-day. There was a letter
and there was a small packet, each with the
cross under the stamp which warned me
not to touch them. There has been nothing
else."

"That may prove quite enough," said

Holmes, grimly. "Now, Mr. Bennett, we
shall, I think, come to some conclusion
to-night. If my deductions are correct we
should have an opportunity of bringing
matters to a head. In order to do so it is
necessary to hold the Professor under
observation. I would suggest, therefore,
that you remain awake and on the look-out.
Should you hear him pass your door do not

grinned and gibbered at us in his senseless
would have had to fight our way out of the
had not intervened.

interrupt him, but follow him as discreetly
as you can. Dr. Watson and I will not be
far off. By the way, where is the key of
that little box of which you spoke ? ''

"Upon his watch-chain."

"I fancy our researches must lie in that
direction. At the worst the lock should not
be very formidable. Have you any other
able-bodied man on the premises ? "

"There is the coach-
man, Macphail."

"Where does he sleep ? "

"Over the stables."

"We might possibly want him. Well, we
can do no more until we see how things
develop. Good-bye—but I expect that we
shall see you before morning."

IT was nearly midnight before we took our
station among some bushes immediately
opposite the hall door of the Professor.
It was a fine night, but chilly, and we were
glad of our warm overcoats. There was a
breeze and clouds were scudding across the

sky, obscuring from time to time the half-moon. It would have been a dismal vigil were it not for the expectation and excitement which carried us along, and the assurance of my comrade that we had probably reached the end of the strange sequence of events which had engaged our attention.

"If the cycle of nine days holds good then we shall have the Professor at his worst to-night," said Holmes. "The fact that these strange symptoms began after his visit to Prague, that he is in secret correspondence with a Bohemian dealer in London, who presumably represents someone in Prague, and that he received a packet from him this very day, all point in one direction. What he takes and why he takes it are still beyond our ken, but that it emanates in some way from Prague is clear enough. He takes it under definite directions which regulate this ninth day system, which was the first point which attracted my attention. But his symptoms are most remarkable. Did you observe his knuckles?"

I had to confess that I did not.

"Thick and horny in a way which is quite new in my experience. Always look at the hands first, Watson. Then cuffs, trouser-knees, and boots. Very curious knuckles which can only be explained by the mode of progression observed by——" Holmes paused, and suddenly clapped his hand to his forehead. "Oh, Watson, Watson, what a fool I have been! It seems incredible, and yet it must be true. All points in one direction. How could I miss seeing the connection of ideas? Those knuckles—how could I have passed those knuckles? And the dog! And the ivy! It's surely time that I disappeared into that little farm of my dreams. Look out, Watson! Here he is! We shall have the chance of seeing for ourselves."

THE hall door had slowly opened, and against the lamp-lit background we saw the tall figure of Professor Presbury. He was clad in his dressing-gown. As he stood outlined in the doorway he was erect but leaning forward with dangling arms, as when we saw him last.

Now he stepped forward into the drive, and an extraordinary change came over him. He sank down into a crouching position, and moved along upon his hands and feet, skipping every now and then as if he were overflowing with energy and vitality. He moved along the face of the house and then round the corner. As he disappeared Bennett slipped through the hall door and softly followed him.

"Come, Watson, come!" cried Holmes, and we stole as softly as we could through the bushes until we had gained a spot whence we could see the other side of the house, which was bathed in the light of the half-moon. The Professor was clearly visible crouching at the foot of the ivy-covered wall. As we watched him he suddenly began with incredible agility to ascend it. From branch to branch he sprang, sure of foot and firm of grasp, climbing apparently in mere joy at his own powers, with no definite object in view. With his dressing-gown flapping on each side of him he looked like some huge bat glued against the side of his own house, a great square dark patch upon the moonlit wall. Presently he tired of this amusement, and, dropping from branch to branch, he squatted down into the old attitude and moved towards the stables, creeping along in the same strange way as before. The wolf-hound was out now, barking furiously, and more excited than ever when it actually caught sight of its master. It was straining on its chain, and quivering with eagerness and rage. The Professor squatted down very deliberately just out of reach of the hound, and began to provoke it in every possible way. He took handfuls of pebbles from the drive and threw them in the dog's face, prodded him with a stick which he had picked up, flicked his hands about only a few inches from the gaping mouth, and endeavoured in every way to increase the animal's fury, which was already beyond all control. In all our adventures I do not know that I have ever seen a more strange sight than this impassive and still dignified figure crouching frog-like upon the ground and goading to a wilder exhibition of passion the maddened hound, which ramped and raged in front of him, by all manner of ingenious and calculated cruelty.

And then in a moment it happened! It was not the chain that broke, but it was the collar that slipped, for it had been made for a thick-necked Newfoundland. We heard the rattle of falling metal, and the next instant dog and man were rolling on the ground together, the one roaring in rage, the other screaming in a strange shrill falsetto of terror. It was a very narrow thing for the Professor's life. The savage creature had him fairly by the throat, its fangs had bitten deep, and he was senseless before we could reach them and drag the two apart. It might have been a dangerous task for us, but Bennett's voice and pressure brought the great wolf-hound instantly to reason. The uproar had brought the sleepy and astonished coachman from his room above the stables. "I'm not surprised," said he, shaking his head. "I've seen him at it before. I knew the dog would get him sooner or later."

Dog and man were rolling on the ground together, the one roaring in rage, the other screaming in a strange shrill falsetto of terror.